Praise for
Remnants of Shadow and Light

"Sias Bryant has written an exhuberant new treasure chest of short fiction. While these stories defy catagorization, at once dark and light, painful and sweet, they resonate with a deep clarity and an even deeper honesty about women's lives. I couldn't recommend this collection more highly."
— Ellen Hart
five time winner of the *Lambda Literary Award*

"Sias Bryant writes with an unerring ear for dialogue and a sensitivity to human emotion. Every story packs a punch and leaves you gasping for air, surprised and amazed by its intensity. Five-star reads all around."
— Lori L. Lake
author of *Stepping Out: Short Stories*

Remnants of
Shadow and
Light

Sias
Bryant

Zerynthia 's Tales 1

Bedazzled Ink Publishing Company * Fairfield, California

978-0-9759555-8-1 paperback
0-9759555-8-6 paperback

First published 2007
cover art and design by C. A. Casey

Nuance Books
a division of
Bedazzled Ink Publishing Company
Fairfield, California
http://www.bedazzledink.com/nuance

To Suzanne
Because you already know

ACKNOWLEDGMENTS

For all of you who have supported me, thought the very best of me, and given me the insight to put voice to paper, I am eternally grateful. You know who you are: brothers, sisters, mothers, fathers, children, and friends, thank you.

Thanks also to Pat and to Lori for encouraging me and holding my emotional feet to the fires of forward motion. Without you, this little book would not have come to pass.

And finally to the women; those I've created in this book and those in the midst of their own transitions. I am in awe of who you are . . . and who you are becoming.

Sias Bryant

"There is a well-written story in every woman. Whether or not she chooses to tell it could likely be the most important decision she ever makes."

Diane Ferreira

Table of Contents

Foreword

How these stories came about is interesting fodder for any therapist but the sequence of events that led to their writing taught me something about transition.

First, there was a death. Then, there was more than one unimaginable betrayal followed by a mass exodus and the loss of a child. Surprisingly enough, as each of these moments took place, I became more reflective and less emotionally visible to the naked eye. As I moved inward and looked for who I might become, the women in these stories were quite often my companions on the road. I breathed life into them, I created their defining moments, and then I chose to leave most of them to make their own decisions about whether to resolve or not, to heal or not. These were the same choices that I had and I became a better woman as I gained awareness about choosing.

When I found Bedazzled Ink, my emotional skin was still raw—some of that my own doing, mind you—but I was no longer bleeding internally. A wonderfully kind and insightful editor thought that my words resonated close to the heart and, since I think that is exactly where words belong, we began this journey together; I am, quite simply, blessed.

The women in these stories are fictional but I am convinced that somewhere their defining moments are happening to someone. That belief keeps me safe and sorry, terrified and tickled. But mostly, it keeps me writing.

June, 2007
Sias Bryant

The Fisher

"Tide goes out and that dingy there will look like it was set in a pile of muck waist deep. Few hours later, she'll be buoying up and over like a raft in a squall."

The sturdy fisher spit the fact through his clenched teeth that held a pipe securely toward the right side of his mouth. He finger-laced a hole in a large net that had recently ripped while hauling crab. He used a fine rope of what looked like shoestring and skillfully weaved the strands of netting until they formed a solid bond across the eighteen-inch hole. The precision of his stitch was impressive and I was mesmerized by his voice. It was a deep and soothing sound that split the eerie morning silence and caused me to hear the salt water bubbling at the back of his throat.

He had worked the boats all his life he said, and his presence proved it to me. His enormous hands were calloused and scarred from years of scraping fish fins. I assumed that the bright orange hat and tan waders held up by suspenders were his daily attire. I thought that the turtleneck shirt underneath looked as though it was only changed when absolutely necessary. The multitude of lines on his face were rugged, much like I assumed the life of a fisher to be. He was such an interesting sight that I forgot for a moment the questions to ask. I had taken leave of my mission and concentrated on his busywork instead.

A silence fell between us and he looked at me with a short smile.

"What are you doin' down here at six bells, Miss?"

The idea that anyone would call me "Miss" was absurd and made me smile inwardly. He was just as comfortable with company as he was with the net. I wanted to pack up his easiness with me somehow so I could remember it after I'd gone.

"I'm visiting here and had not yet seen the bay side. Thought I'd come and take a look before another tourist came around and spoiled my view."

We both then turned from each other and stared collectively at the sea. The bay was sized well enough to bring in several large fishing boats and, in its day, had probably done just that. The long boardwalk from the center of town now mostly housed whale watching tour boats on its right. The few remaining fishing boats on the left were well-worn and snug in their watery spaces. They lulled me with a creaking sound in their bellies that was a haunting consolation. The view from the end of the pier was an exercise in opposites. To the left, beyond the boats, was the sleepy town that stretched along the waterline and formed the arc of the bay. Straight ahead was the rock wall breaker, distant and vigilant in protecting the bay's inner cargo against the elements of the sea. And directly to the right was the reason I had come to the dock that morning.

There were four salt-stained pictures displayed side by side that ran the height of the oversized boathouse. The individual photo-like images made a quartet of grandmotherly women staring beyond the bay, keeping watch over the tiny town. I remembered why I had set the alarm and walked the pier that morning. I turned toward the side of the boathouse and spoke to my companion.

"Can you tell me about those pictures?"

He dropped his head toward his shoes as if he'd lost something. Then, moving his gaze up to my face, he caught my glance and held it. Honestly, I couldn't see a difference between his eyes and the color of the sea behind him.

"I can."

He still fixed his stare into me and I breathed a steady rhythm while waiting for his next words.

"What's your name, Miss?"

"Diane."

He smiled at the sound of my name and softy spoke a word that I couldn't hear.

"I'm sorry, sir, didn't hear you."

He turned his gaze toward the women and said, "Tokias. Long 'i.' Tok-eye-us." Then he turned toward me and continued, "That's my name."

Pause.

"What interests you about 'em, Miss?"

"Diane, please, sir."

"Tokias, please, Miss."

We both grinned at one another and let the moment of familiarity sit between us until I finally spoke.

"I guess I am intrigued by their presence. Who are they? And who decided they should be up on the boathouse for fishers and travelers coming in by ferry to see?"

"Those women were the beacon of hope for the men who fished. They stood and kept the town safe until their men came home from sea. At least three of them did."

"Why only three?"

Tokias gazed again toward the sea and then back to me. "Would you like ta' come aboard? Coffee?"

"That'd be great. It's freezing out here."

The fisher reached out to take my arm as I steadied myself on one of the dock's massive timber pylon supports. His watery fingers and firm grip dwarfed my hands as he guided me neatly onto the boat. The vessel had to be known around the tiny town as a rust bucket. Worn and faded paint on the stern looked like the boat must've been named after its present owner. The "T O K", and "I" were barely visible and the "A" and "S" were only partially remaining. Its masts, paintless and weathered, were streaked with a color like red autumn leaves and her ropes were charcoal gray and frayed. The black shoulder of the starboard bow had a six foot crease running parallel to the water that had been patched recently. There were three hatches that tanked the fish and a small cabin was just above the one closest to the rear. Tokias stepped into the cabin and returned with two cups and an ancient percolator pot.

"Anything in it?"

"No, black's good, thanks. How old is this boat?"

"Old enough, I reckon. You married?"

I smiled and wondered how the old guy would take the news. "No. I've had a woman in my life for the last twenty years, though."

He didn't flinch or move a muscle. That was either a really good or really bad sign.

"Then you've got more in common with Elizabeth than I thought," Tokias said. He gestured toward the women on the boathouse.

"Which one is Elizabeth?"

"Second one there on the left."

The woman in the painting was about seventy years old with kind, wide-set eyes. Her white hair was pulled back and away from her face. The look she cast seemed determined, even vigilant, but not stern. Elizabeth's neck and face were weathered in the same way that

Tokias and the townspeople were—leathered and brown from the sun and rain.

"She's beautiful." I waited a moment while we both stared at Elizabeth, then asked, "Did her husband know? That she was a lesbian, I mean."

Tokias puffed on his pipe and smiled ever so slightly. "Yeah, I reckon so."

I sat with my cup on the massive ropes piled at the stern and waited for him to continue. Tokias finally turned away from the boathouse and toward me. He leaned against the side of the boat, coffee and pipe in hand, and began.

"Time was when this town was not as acceptin' as it is now. Back then," he gestured toward the women's portraits, "men brought their women here to keep a home for them to come to when fishin' was up for the week. Now, everything's different, course, and prob'ly for the better, I'd say. Anyway, Elizabeth and the person everybody thought was her husband, Pal—short for Palance, came out here in the spring one year. They were hopin' ta' get a purse full a' money from the lobster runs and then move in ta' Boston. She was a lady and Pal was a drifter, at least, until Elizabeth came along. Once they had found each other, all they could think of was gettin' away from Fall River. After a few seasons here, they came to love it and stayed on."

"What do you mean 'everybody thought Pal was her husband'? Weren't they married?"

"Not in the usual sense, no. They couldn't marry because Pal was not a man. Do you want me to tell this story or not?"

"Sorry."

"Pal was a runaround, no-good, handsome, devil-dog that didn't deserve Elizabeth for one minute. He . . . er . . . she cleaned up her ways, though, when she fell in love with the smartest girl in Fall River and that was Elizabeth. Who coulda thought such a thing in 1887?" Before he raised his voice any louder, Tokias paused and drew a deep breath. Exhaling, he began to pack his pipe and started to speak again. "Pal was no match for Elizabeth but Elizabeth loved her just the same. Love balances out most unequal things about livin', I guess.

"Anyhow, the story goes that they met in Fall River in 1886 at the home of a wealthy fella, Malachi Cross, who was a lumber baron there in town. He was in love with Elizabeth and wanted to impress her so he threw a ball in his big mansion. He invited everyone he could think of so that she might think him impressive, or at least, generous.

"Well, the whole town turned out to what soon became known as the gala of the century. The nineteen-year-old Elizabeth had never been to a ball before and was excited enough to go but didn't care a fig for the forty-year-old Malachi Cross. Course, nobody really knew that at all. Feelings and such were not discussed much then, I reckon. It didn't seem to matter how she felt anyway 'cause her parents loved Malachi and his money enough to encourage the romance whether she wanted it or not.

"I've heard tell that there was never a more beautiful night for a dance. As the sun glowed its way into the belly of the earth, torches were lit for a mile up the road from the baron's place. People came in carriages, on horses, and afoot. They came in pairs and groups and families from as far away as fifty miles. Now the actual number has been lost over the years as to how many there might've been but the ballroom was believed to have held seven hundred and fifty people. The music and the food musta cost a fortune back then and Malachi had done it all for a young lady who barely knew he was alive. There were butlers and wine stewards and, more important, a fortune teller in a parlor off the main hall. It was carnival atmosphere all right and Elizabeth was having herself quite a time. Malachi, on the other hand, could not get a word in with her since he had so many guests to tend to. Elizabeth finally begged off from the watchful eyes of her parents and wandered into the dimly lit parlor of the fortune teller.

"Now, here's the thing.

"Lots of folks have told the story that Elizabeth was bewitched that night by this fortune tellin' lady. She's been described as a spectacular woman with unusual handsomeness about her. Her eyes were steel blue and known to cut even the most aristocratic folks to the quick when she read their futures to them. She could see through almost everybody, they say, and she was quite the character in her gypsy clothes with bells around her ankles. I guess her voice was just about the most melodic sound anybody had ever heard and, that night, people were lined up outside the open door of the parlor to see her. Well, when the fortune teller noticed Elizabeth at the back of the line, she flew out of her chair, almost knockin' over her gazin' ball and other tellin' things she'd brought with her. She hurried her to the front and told everyone else they'd have to wait and then closed the door behind them. What happened in there was anybody's guess and there's been a fair amount of speculation since then, that's for sure. Whatever it was, when Elizabeth came outta that parlor an hour or so later, she was a changed girl. I reckon I believe that she wouldn't have gotten involved with Pal or come out here if not for that fortune tellin' lady."

As I listened to Tokias paint the picture of Elizabeth and Pal, I heard a bell from another boat ringing in the distance. He glanced once toward the seawall then looked at me squarely.

"Fog won't lift for a time. That's what the bell's for. More coffee?"

"Yes. Please. So, when did Elizabeth and Pal meet that night?"

Tokias poured the steaming brew into her half-empty mug. "Well, it musta been close to the end of the evening because Elizabeth's mother and sisters had already gone home. Mr. Cross had assured Elizabeth's mother that she would be brought home by his carriage before midnight. At the stroke of twelve o'clock, however, Elizabeth was no where to be found."

"But I thought that—"

"Just hang on now and I'll tell ya'. Pal came into Cross's party at the invitation of a business associate or so it's told. No one knew him and no one could tell that he was not a 'he' at all."

"But if no one could tell then how do you know he was really not a 'he'?" I interrupted.

"Lord, you talk a lot for someone who wants to learn a story."

"Sorry."

"The truth o' the matter is that no one knew in the beginnin' *or* the end."

I hesitated. "End of what?"

"End o' Pal's life."

"Well, how'd he die?"

Annoyed, Tokias replied, "What say I finish telling ya' about his livin' first?"

"Sorry."

"Now, where was I? Right, yes, well . . . let me see. Pal came in at the end of the evening, spotted Elizabeth from fifty feet away and I guess he never took his eyes from her. When Elizabeth saw Pal from every corner of the room, starin' at her with such intent that she finally approached him. She said in a clear voice so that all could hear, 'Have we met, sir? For if we have, I am at such a loss. I am puzzled by your gaze and impudence as I do not recall ever making your acquaintance.' Well, instead of being put off by her words, Pal gathered Elizabeth's hand into his own and softly kissed it as he uttered these astonishing words. 'It was you who summoned me, Miss Elizabeth, through this very hand that you placed earlier into that of a fortune teller.' Well, the room was first quiet as a church then all buzz broke loose as word of his reply spread. No one could quite understand just how Pal knew about Elizabeth's fortune telling experience. Some believed that he was a magician and somehow connected to the teller but the woman insisted that he was not. After hearing Pal's ominous words, Elizabeth turned the whitest shade of milk. Her eyes burned into his face until the room seemed barely big enough to hold them. The heat in that room between the two of them was fuel for a barn load of gossip. Word about the moment of their meeting was spread throughout the county for weeks. Nobody had ever heard of Pal but most everybody wanted to see the man who had captured Elizabeth's heart. Malachi Cross was sure upset but Elizabeth was clear that Pal would be her choice. Oh, she didn't say it in so many words but those who knew her were convinced that she would make the decision to follow Pal to the ends of the earth if she had to."

"Sounds like a lesbian relationship," I muttered.

The old man crooked his neck and cupped his ear. "What say?"

"Oh, I . . . nothing. Did Elizabeth know Pal was a woman that night?"

"Well, that's a fair question. I would reckon that she somehow knew from the minute she laid eyes on her."

I pondered my relationship with Grace for a moment; how I loved her and how close we were. I wonder if I could've ever mistaken her for a man. More to the point, could she have mistaken me for a man? I looked down at my sizable breasts and wide hips. Not likely.

"Why do you think that, Tokias? Maybe she didn't know until she had already fallen in love with him . . . her."

"Love's a funny thing, isn't it? We search for someone everywhere and then try everybody on for size like a new coat. No gender in a pattern o' threads sewn together, is there? Truth is, we usually don't find love until we're deep in thought about somethin' else entirely, ya' know? Maybe it's the laundry or a grocery list we're thinkin' about when the tide shifts or the winds change. Then someone we never thought we'd meet shows up when we're doin' something else like foldin' a favorite shirt or standin' in the bread aisle." Tokias leaned into the side of the boat, hands in his pockets, and stared out at the water in the bay.

"Are you saying that the most memorable moments we encounter are ushered in to us by our menial tasks? Sounds like an accident to me."

"It may very well be, Diane, that's the greatest accident we'll ever possess fortune enough to have. What I'm sayin' is, accident or not, Elizabeth had no more intention of meetin' the person she would love for the rest of her life than meetin' the man in the moon." Tokias again packed his pipe and allowed the words to float into the fog and out to sea. Finally he asked, "Do you love your woman then?"

"Grace? Yes, of course, I do."

"Then have ya' ever considered what you might do for her? 'Cause that was the question for Elizabeth in those days. She did come to know that Pal was a woman and she had ta' decide every day if the love she felt would outweigh the complete rejection she'd face if anybody found out. It was a hard choice, girl. Not many people back then were understandin' things like these days." The fisher caught himself before he raised his voice to a louder pitch and softened a bit. "O' course, it wasn't like ya' could see underneath all the finery they wore either. Pal was strappin' big and with a little binding around the chest, no one was the wiser. She'd shaved since she was twelve," then added, "least that's what I've heard tell."

"Can you tell me more about where they lived? How they died?"

Tokias squinted into his coffee cup. "Pal took Elizabeth into his arms that very night and began a whirlwind courtship. When Elizabeth disappeared from the party, the gossip was that Pal had spent the whole night convincin' her ta' leave Fall River. I like to think that were just takin' their first steps in time together. Like any two people given the gift of creatin' a separate life, they marveled at the breath of one another. Come sunrise, Pal was just walkin' Elizabeth in her parents' door. Well, that didn't go over so well and although her parents were kindly people, they were also upset that Elizabeth had not given Mr. Cross his due time with her. After all, what would people think about their only daughter leaving the party given for her with a stranger? Oh, if they only known the half of it! They surely woulda perished right then and there." Tokias laughed loud and hard until I finally spoke.

"You're a strange man, Tokias. You know that, right?"

"Aye, I do. Anyway, Elizabeth couldn't reason with her parents and Pal couldn't wait. A few weeks after the gala of the century, Elizabeth ran away from Fall River and into the arms of Pal. They came out to this end of the earth so that Pal could work the boats. It was here at City Hall they married."

"You mean, like, *married* married? *The* marriage that I am currently forbidden to have in these United States, present state excluded? *That* marriage?"

"Tell me, Diane, do you really think that same-sex marriage was dreamed up in the last twenty or thirty years? My guess is that the righteous of this world would explode halfway up to heaven if they had any inkling of the number of marriages between women that were performed. Men too, I reckon." Tokias bit the pipe between his teeth as another fog horn blew into the soupy bay. "Not long now."

I couldn't see an end to the fog at all but, then again, I am no fisher. I stared up at Elizabeth and admired her devotion. Tokias began to speak again.

"For years, she walked Pal to the docks every day and then went about her chores. Toward sunset, she'd come down and wait for Pal each evenin'. Her arms folded as she paced, she'd tuck a wisp of hair behind her ear ever so often. She'd stare just over that rock wall to watch for the boats to come in loaded with fish. It was like she knew somethin' bad would happen at some point. Fishin' was a bit more dangerous back then. No radar or weather channel to forecast a sudden storm or other tragedy."

I studied the fisher for a moment before I spoke. "You seem to know a lot about these folks, Tokias. How did you find out about Pal being a woman, for instance?"

The fisher fixed his eyes on mine and spoke carefully. "Folklore around here is all us ol' timers have to pass the time, girl. The youngsters, like you, have taken over the town and rightfully so or there'd be no town, is my guess. We got nothin' more than tales to spin. Who knows how much is really true after all these years 'cept that Pal was female." After a moment, he added, "That's a fact for sure."

"What did you mean when you said that Elizabeth acted like she knew something bad would happen?"

Tokias lowered his voice and clenched his teeth around the pipe for effect.

"Well, see, the fog was just about as bad as it could get that morning when Pal's boat went out. I reckon that the Captain figured that it'd burn off by midday and he couldn't waste a mornin' just sewin' net with two other men needin' ta' work. They settled for goin' out on the bayside here to check the lobster crates before headin' out. Elizabeth was right here that mornin'," Tokias pointed toward the end of the dock, "and I've heard tell she was mighty upset that Pal wouldn't stay off that boat. After a few private words, he jumped on-board, calling to shore that he'd see her that evenin'. Elizabeth never left the dock that day and the fog never lifted. Along about eight o'clock, it was pitch black and Elizabeth began to call out for Pal into the soup. There was not a noise to be heard 'cept the lap of the water against the pylons." Tokias now began to whisper. "To this day, you can sometimes hear her voice callin' to Pal in the sound of the sea bells." The fisher waited a moment before resuming his story.

"Boat was alee and drifted in close enough to be towed by a tug waitin' out a mile or two. Had a hole in her starboard side the size of a marlin and nobody could figure out what they'd hit. Deck was quiet and nobody on-board but the junior mate, stumblin' over his words and talkin' to himself. The boy had turned idiot and kept screamin' then runnin' and pointin' to the fish hatches. Well, the tug Captain climbed aboard and opened the hatch."

Tokias stood staring wide-eyed at the hatches on his own boat.

"Well? Come on! What was in there?" I waited.

"Pal was in there. Least they believe it was him. It was the bottom half of a torso, wearin' Pal's torn pants and shoes. His hat was floatin' in there, too."

"My God, what had happened?"

"Lots o' speculation but the story that was told is Pal had gone overboard and was bit clean in half by an unusually large shark. When the Captain and the boy fished him out, they were surprised to see that half a' Pal was missin' and the other half was exposed enough to tell 'em that their mate had also lost an important member of his body." Tokias was as straight-faced as a judge.

"You're kidding, right?"

"As I sit right here, I swear on my dead wife's grave that's the story that was told."

"And you believe it?"

"Well, what I believe isn't really what counts, I reckon." Tokias tapped his pipe and began loading it again. "It's a good 'nough story."

"Is it? Reee-aaally?" I skeptically eyed my companion.

Tokias glanced sideways toward me. "I think that the truth o' the matter is that none of us would really want to know the truth o' the matter."

"Meaning?"

"Meanin' that Captain may have been a rigid and mean bastard; that when he spied on Pal takin' a leak over the side without male equipment that day, he may have gutted him like a fish and fed the upper half o' him to the sea. Maybe the other half he was bringin' in ta' parade around like a freak show for the whole town ta' see."

The thought of Pal's naked torso being on display made my body shake. "But that didn't happen, right? Nobody knew Pal was a woman."

"Naw, didn't happen. I told ya' the secret stayed safe. The tug Captain got caught in a squall and nobody found the boat or the tug for days. Only one saved was the boy on the boat but he stayed crazy as a bedbug. He told how Pal was bit in half and had no . . . part . . . ya' know but I reckon folks thought he lost it in the shark attack. Most of the story was gossip and folly, anyhow."

Tokias began to wind the waterlogged rope that was attached to the anchor. A foghorn blew three short bursts from the bayside. The fisher looked to me as if to say it was time for him to go.

I stood to leave. "So, how did Elizabeth die?"

"Like any other woman who loved her mate that much, she died of a broken heart, I reckon." Tokias gestured toward the picture. "The town loved Elizabeth. That's why she's still there." Tokias put his huge hands out to help me onto the dock. The feel of his watery skin made me want to cry, somehow.

"Maybe I'll see you again before I leave, Tokias. I appreciate you sharing the story of Elizabeth with me and telling me about her courage. I'm glad that she's up there."

"Aye, Diane, I'm glad as well. Best to you and your Missus, girl."

I watched Tokias' boat sputter backward into the bay before turning toward open water. He turned back once to salute a final wave as the rear of the boat disappeared into the fog. I waited until the name on his boat faded from sight then headed down the dock.

A few slips down, three fishers were gathering tackle and tossing nets on their boat. As I emerged from the haze, the three glanced up.

"Mornin'," they muttered.

"Morning, gentlemen. Almost ready to go out?"

One young fisher with a yellow-slicker and wool hat replied, "Not today. Fog's too thick. We'll repair nets since we're socked in 'til sometime tomorrow."

"But . . . but I just watched a boat go out."

The men on the boat glanced at one another then back toward me. The slicker spoke again. "Are you sure?" He turned to his buddy. "Can't imagine anyone would go out in this soup. Did you catch the name of the boat or its Captain?"

"Actually, I believe that the boat and the Captain have the same name. Tokias. I don't know his last name. Do you know him?"

All motion seemed to stop on the boat and the fishers came over to me to get a better look. "Tokias?" A tall and bearded fisher looked as if he questioned my sanity. "Only Tokias around here wasn't a first name. It was the last name of a fisher and his wife, Elizabeth. She's up there on the boathouse, there, second from the left." He pointed to the woman's picture and continued, "Her husband's name was—"

"Palance," I interrupted.

"Yeah, how'd you know? Folks called him Pal, for short. He's part of the folklore 'round here. Story goes that in 1938, he lost his, well, his . . . you know . . . member . . . from a shark bite that also cut him in half. Kid on the boat that saw it happen went crazy. Legend says that you can still hear his wife Elizabeth—"

Again I finished his sentence. "Calling to Pal in the sound of the sea bells."

The fishers were watching me with great interest as I hurried to the end of the dock and attempted to study the milky horizon. There was little visibility; still I strained to see any sign or shadow of Tokias's boat. I saw nothing but thought I heard a distinctive voice faintly calling while the sea bells began to echo in the mist.

Crew of One

The ground was clay, rich and wet, with veins of sienna-colored stripes winding through its black core. Shovel in, shovel out, earth upon earth.

Kenna McIntyre tossed out spades of dirt from a dark crevice to make room for a stranger's silent rest. The sound of snapping branches in the wind signaled a quickly approaching shower. There was a lot to do before the rain came.

She scrambled out of the hole from an old wooden ladder propped on the north end of the grave. She covered the ground just around the hollow with a tarp that would keep it from collapsing on itself, or on her, for that matter. When she was satisfied that the covering was in place, she staked the edges with urns from the burial truck.

She carried the flower urns just in case there were broken or missing ones on other graves along the way to her digging site for the day. One by one as they disappeared or somehow became damaged, Kenna replaced them with one of the oversized vases from her boss's pick-up. Lowery had warned her not to do that.

"Those urns are for new, paying customers, McIntyre. The old, penniless ones don't give a shit."

Kenna didn't see it that way.

Next, she took a twenty pound bag of sand, ripped it open, and poured a quarter of it into a weighty bucket. Walking carefully around the perimeter, she spread a thin layer of beach into the tomb. It was much easier to throw wet sand than it was to bail out the mud. After five years of digging, she knew the secrets of the trade. When to run for cover, whether or not the ground was safe to sink into, how to best finish what the backhoe had started; these were all measurements of wisdom she had acquired, one spade full at a time.

She dropped onto the edge of the grave and let her feet dangle over the hole. The shower would last fifteen minutes or so from the look of the sky. She preferred to sit in the rain and watch the sand plump up from the brief downpour rather than take shelter in the truck.

When she had worked with other diggers, they thought she was crazy.

"What's the matter with you? Once you're soaked, you'll freeze your ass off out there."

Kenna was mystified about why they would care where she chose to sit.

Gravediggers work in crews. When she went to Lowery and asked to work alone, that's what he had said. Maybe it was because she stood stoically inside the door of his office with no sign of leaving that changed his mind. Or maybe it was because her unique brand of silent strength secretly frightened him, somehow. Whatever it was, Lowery made a different decision than he ever had and gave her a truck of her own along with a separate digging assignment. Pinned up on the project board each morning, Kenna's name fell under the heading, "Crew of One."

Taking a deep breath, she drummed the watch on her left wrist with her right forefinger while she stared aimlessly into the grave. The tapping was a habit that she developed years ago. Whenever she was confused about life or emotionally embroiled in some way, especially with Allison, her mother, Kenna had learned to use her watch as a touchstone. The gentle cadence had kept her occupied while her friends talked about boys and cheerleading. It also provided distraction when her mother made another useless attempt to convince her daughter not to be with a woman. The watch face had saved many a vase from flying through a window or toward a slamming door. Now, Kenna drummed the time piece to keep comfort from those graceless memories; little raps of rhythm that soothed her somehow and brought order into her solitude.

It was close to 11:30 a.m. and Kenna thought about her afternoon assignment. The Pickerson funeral was at nine tomorrow and she was sure that the backhoe had already completed that plot. When she finished up there, Sewell was next on the east end, then Hobart by the chapel.

She remembered each digging place not by number, as other diggers did, but by name. When she worked, she imagined the lives of these now-dead strangers as books of history; pages of families and friends held together by ominously fateful beginnings and endings. Her somewhat personal attachment may have seemed odd to an outsider but, to Kenna, her musings about those in her charge were a necessary task of the job. Without personalizing the dead, she would simply be making holes in the earth. As it was, she put them to rest with tidy stories of closure and it gave her comfort to do so. In her mind, the Pickersons and Hobarts of the world were admirable people with productive lives and good intentions who were loved by all. Kenna burrowed the ground and concocted unfamiliar lives of perfection for those waiting to be lowered into her graves.

She mentally eulogized each of the deceased with a flawless tale of courage and success. The lie was abominable, she knew, but the dead were grateful for her tributes. Most people were really pathetic and lost; barely worthy of her service.

She tapped her watch face once again and breathed in time with its second hand.

Rain spattered the dirt around her and she lifted her face skyward. The drops of moisture on her face suddenly reminded her of the last time she had cried. Hunkering further into her chosen spot, she allowed herself to think of someone aside from the dead. Someone she actually knew. Someone she loved.

Brit Harris.

Soft-handed, sweet smiling, tongue-in-cheek, Brit. Her voice, with a slight south Boston accent, rolled over in Kenna's memory and she felt her jaw clench. Although she tried to stop it there, the inevitable happened and a vision of Brit relentlessly surfaced. Soon enough Kenna saw the dark hair that tumbled onto her chest and sea-blue eyes fluttering awake next to her. The last time she had seen those eyes, she thought that what she had seen was happiness. Nothing could've been further from the truth, apparently. Maybe there had been someone else but that was unlikely. Chances are that Brit had fallen out of love with her and was too kind to say so. One day she was gone, leaving a two sentence, oddly scrawled note that Kenna kept in the top drawer of her dresser.

It said, "You are greater than anything I had ever hoped could happen to me. Who would've asked for more? B.H." Since Brit had no family, Kenna didn't know where to search for her.

No tidy story of closure there.

The note and Brit's whereabouts were a mystery that, after a while, Kenna had stopped trying to solve. Besides, Brit wasn't the only woman she had lost. Her first love, Sheila, had left her as well. She was so sure that the young girl had loved her but just before Kenna's eighteenth birthday, Sheila fled their little town. A few weeks later,

Kenna received a package from Chicago. Enclosed was the copy of her favorite book, *Leaves of Grass*, that she had given to Sheila months before. No return address. Sheila's parents had frantically searched for their youngest daughter until a letter arrived from Chicago on the same day as Kenna's book. And still, no return address.

Kenna eventually came to believe that she knew why neither woman could stay with her. They had grown tired of her brooding silence and peculiar ways. She was odd and she knew it but couldn't find ways to express it; a deadly pathology for relationships, she deduced. What other reason would they have left?

Losing the women she loved created a dense complexity in Kenna that caused most people to avoid her. A haunting slice of memory cut raw and deep into her every intention. Anyone around her could see that she was wounded dangerously close to her heart. People assessed her as oddly treacherous and stepped away from her dense silence and ominous eyes.

"She's nuts, man . . ."

"You right about that . . ."

"She needs some help . . ."

"Certifiable . . ."

"Yeah, crazy . . ."

Kenna almost smiled when she thought of how others judged her. Maybe she would dig one of their graves someday. She might enjoy constructing tidy stories about any one of them.

The rain stopped at 11:50 and she propped the ladder against the east wall of the hole. Kenna had to keep moving if she was going to leave before dusk. She had agreed to meet her mother after work even though she had barely spoken to her for almost a year. Allison avoided her, she knew that. In fact, Kenna most always attempted to return the favor. Her mother would never accept her and it was certain that she would never accept a woman in her life. Kenna would bet that Allison somehow knew Brit had left or she wouldn't have called and asked to see her only child. Her mother would see Brit's departure as an opportunity for her to again see if she could get Kenna to come home to live. Allison wanted her to stop loving women. She wanted her to be someone that Kenna detested; someone like her. When Kenna had lived at home, her mother had the same agenda after Sheila disappeared from her life. Allison tried to get close to her in any way she could. Less like a mother than a competitor, she wanted to monopolize Kenna's every living moment; she desperately wanted to touch her in profound ways that would change her very core. When

Kenna imagined her mother's frantic gestures, the air around her became thick and lifeless.

Her chest tightened as the watch face echoed under her fingers; tap . . . tap . . . tap.

Finally, descending into the earthy comfort, she centered her attention on finishing the grave. The recollection of Brit and her mother was fading and Kenna shook the remnants back into their dormant places. She ran the long spade down the side of the black hole and gathered a mixture of sand and dirt. Just as she was about to toss the last bit of ground into the bucket for lifting, a familiar voice startled her from above.

"How's it goin' down there, McIntyre?" Lowery bellowed.

"Ass," Kenna muttered under her breath.

"What say, McIntyre?" Lowery asked.

She took a deep breath to bridle her own response and then simply looked up and out of the hole.

"After lunch, stop by the office, will ya'? I got a new assignment that just came in a few minutes ago. Other crews are busier than hell and we got a quick one comin' in."

Kenna smiled inwardly. That meant he was getting a kickback. When the local coroner had to bury an indigent, they always called Lowery. County would slip him a few bucks to hurry and get the body in the ground before the media could get wind of some drunk being hit by a train or knifed for his coat. It was an almost-shady practice that kept Lowery in beer money at least once a month.

"One o'clock," she replied.

Turning to go, Lowery shouted over his shoulder, "And, dammit, don't use any more of those urns, McIntyre."

Kenna listened for the boss's truck to pull away before turning back to put the finishing touches in the grave. The finish was her favorite part of the job at the cemetery; a perfectly tidy rectangle ready to inhale the remains of a soulless shell. She knew that her work was sanctified by those who left before her. Those now dead wisely appreciated Kenna in ways that the near-stupid living never would.

She cleaned her tools and leaned back onto her truck to inspect her accomplishment. While her gaze fixed upon the hole in the earth, her mind wandered to the flawless peace that death brought. She remembered that someone would dig for her one day; a thought that left her both sad and relieved.

Later that afternoon, Kenna slipped into Lowery's office and stood quietly in the doorway. She saw her boss thoroughly engrossed in a magazine and finally cleared her throat to announce her arrival. Startled, Lowery jumped out of his seat, spilling coffee into his lap and down his tan trouser legs. He scrambled for paper towels to clean up the mess and bellowed, "Goddamit, McIntyre! You scared the hell outta me. Why don't you make some noise, for Chrissake?"

Kenna did not speak but simply met his gaze and waited. Lowery stopped dabbing his crotch and tried to stare back but could not manage the discomfort. He examined the damage to his pants and said, "Ok, well, I'm fine." Kenna smiled almost imperceptibly. She couldn't have cared less how he was. Lowery shifted his weight from one foot to the other.

"So I want you to go down past the Burroughs crypt and in that small plot in back of the mower shed, right next to the train tracks, I want you to dig in. It's only a small pine box but the backhoe can't get down there so it'll take you a while. Best get started." Lowery started toward the door but stopped and froze when he saw Kenna standing so still.

Kenna raised an eyebrow and waited.

"What is it? You can get down there, right? We gotta get her in today, pal."

Lowery danced from one leg to the next, cueing Kenna to move out the door. Kenna glanced around the trailer and blew out a deep breath.

"Well, come on, McIntyre! We gotta roll."

Kenna thrust her hands in her pockets and bored a hole into the space between Lowery's eyes.

"Name?" she whispered.

"What? What say?"

"I need the name . . . of the person."

"For Chrissake, Kenna, what the—? I don't have time for this bullshit! I'm sure that the coroner will have something with him when he delivers the body but I don't know that shit."

Lowery saw that his tirade was lost on her and tried a new tactic. "Look, Kenna, I can't wait to get this hole dug. She's gonna be here in an hour and we gotta have a place to put her because she has been out in the elements, so to speak, for a while. Gimme a break, will ya'? I don't know who she is."

The two stared at one another while Lowery took in a deep breath.

"Ok. I'll tell you what. Let me call down there and see if she had any ID or anything on her. Maybe we can find something out over the phone. Will that work?"

After five years of knowing her customers' names, Kenna was not about to bury a stranger. She nodded and leaned against the wall, crossing her arms.

"Ok, ok. Let me find the number."

As Lowery dialed the phone, Kenna absently tapped the face of her watch with her forefinger.

"Don? Lowery here. Say listen, you got a name on that chick you're sendin' out? No, no problem . . . just for my records, you know? First name? I'll take anything ya' got." Lowery put his hand over the phone. "He's checkin'."

"Yeah, I'm here. No ID? Yeah, what? No, I . . . well, yeah, I guess. Where'd you find that? Sure, ok. I'll just use that then, thanks."

Lowery cradled the phone and hurried over to the door. "Ok, it looks like there was no ID but there was a book in the back pocket of her jeans. I guess the front cover of the book was gone but the first page had a name in it. Says the book belonged to a 'Brit Harris.'"

The reality of hearing Brit's name suddenly weighed on Kenna's chest. She shook her head, blinked, and then blinked again. "What?"

Before he could speak, Kenna headed out the door and toward her truck.

"Wait!" Lowery cried. "We need to bury this damn body, McIntyre! Where are you goin'?"

Kenna slowed her pace and considered his question. She had no idea. Besides, if the body was Brit, she needed to know. She shoved both hands in her pockets and turned toward her boss. Silently, she walked past him to the steps of the doorway and sat down.

Tap, tap, tap, the glass on her wrist shone white in the sun.

For several moments, Lowery paced between the door and Kenna's truck while she watched the road leading into the cemetery. "Where the fuck's that hearse?" he muttered.

Just as Kenna started to stand, the silver coffin car pulled into the lot and she sprang to her feet and hurried to the back door of the hearse. The small and bird-like man climbed out of the driver's seat as Kenna opened the door.

"Whoa, whoa, there buddy . . . sorry . . . lady," the bird said, "I'll get to it. You got a lightning bug here, Lowery. What's the hurry?"

"You got me, Stan."

Kenna stared down the bird and asked, "Her things?"

"What things?" both men wanted to know.

"Her personals . . . where?" Kenna hissed.

"In the front seat. Jeez, it's a few dollars and an old copy of *Leaves of Grass* without a front cover."

"I want the book." Kenna's voice quivered, dangerously close to cracking.

Neither man spoke; they simply watched her struggle to keep her wits about her.

"What's up, McIntyre? It's just a book."

"Fuck you, Lowery," she snapped.

"Ay, oh, what's that? You want to tell me what's goin' on or do you wanna pick up your paycheck elsewhere next week."

Kenna weighed her options and studied Lowery to determine if he was serious before answering. Finally, she drew in a deep breath and softly uttered, "I knew her."

The driver reached into the front seat and produced the coverless book before quietly backing away from Kenna. The two men awkwardly exchanged glances as they moved toward the hearse while she picked up a spade and headed for her truck. Both vehicles winded along the narrow paths until they reached the furthest east point in the cemetery just a few yards from the train tracks. Lowery and the driver unloaded the coffin on the soft dirt and turned to go as Kenna began to dig furiously without gloves; shovel in, shovel out, earth upon earth. For hours, she perfected the shape of the rectangle while sweat poured from her face and blood seeped from the cracks on her hands. For the first time since she became a digger, Kenna invented no tale of flawlessness, no picture-perfect scenario for a lifeless soul. Instead, she became the pathetic and lost, unworthy to dig the grave of her dead lover.

Finally, alone and on her knees, she fingered the knots on the pine box that sat next to the freshly dug hole. Her breath came in quick, haggard bursts as she willed herself to open the lid. The cuts on her hands and fingers stung when she pushed the top off of the casket onto the ground.

Brit. The lifeless body in the box was the same one that Kenna had once held and loved so completely. As she touched the hollowed and blank face, it was evident that Brit had been dead for more than a few days.

"No, no, no," she whispered as she dropped silent tears onto the dead woman's chest and shoulders. Wave after wave of sorrowful sounds crashed through Kenna until she finally rested her pounding and spent head on the edge of her lover's coffin.

After a while, she reached into her back pocket and pulled the coverless copy of *Leaves of Grass* from her hip. Kenna thought about how she had fallen in love with Whitman's classic novel and had loved giving the book to Sheila when they were in high school. After Sheila had left and sent the book back to her, Kenna read it again and again, recapturing the feelings that she had once felt for her first lover. When Kenna fell in love for the second time in her life, it seemed only fitting that she pass the book on to her new partner. Brit had practically memorized each page, reading the pages daily, and then carefully placing the book on her nightstand just before bed. The last time Kenna had seen the paperback, it's well-worn cover intact and lying on the dresser, was the last time she had seen Brit as well. When she came home after work that day, Brit and the book were gone. She slipped the book back into her pocket.

Kenna stood over the mound of freshiy piled dirt and watched the train move slowly past. As the sunset slid down the west side of the graveyard, she took two of the urns off her truck and placed one on either side of Brit's grave. She filled them with soil to keep them grounded and softly twisted them into the earth until they felt securely planted.

She then climbed into her truck and thought about taking up smoking again.

Kenna stared over the grave and into the dusk as her fingernails rapped the timepiece on her arm.

She was uncertain about whether to leave Brit alone in the unmarked grave. The ache in her chest commanded her to stay. But her bones creaked with memory and threatened to turn to dust. The rumble of anger chided her thoughts as she imagined all of the awful things that may have happened to this woman she loved.

Twice in her life Kenna had surfaced from the periphery to move toward someone who might save her from her own odd destiny. At that moment, she felt the weight of all she had lost and the axis of her earth shifted ever-so-slightly. She started the truck and then shut it off again.

The moon blended the bathing light of day into a cool shower of blue and inky night. Fireflies danced to the crickets' mating call and Kenna imagined that Brit would love the sight and sound of their living. She also thought about Sheila and her sweet, loving face. Lost in the past, Kenna was not aware of the familiar car that pulled next to her truck in the back part of the cemetery. She blinked toward the grave, then looked to her passenger's side, and saw her mother waiting next to the truck in her car. Kenna slipped her keys out of the ignition and stepped into the warm night.

Shaking her head slowly, she knew that she could not spend more than a moment making an excuse for breaking the plans. If she did, she might fall apart or, worse, tell her mother the reason that she needed to be alone. The truth was not something that she could ever entrust to Allison.

Allison rolled down the driver's window and spoke from the dark car. "Hello, darling! How are you on this beautiful summer's night? Glorious, isn't it? Shall we get you cleaned up and grab a bite to eat? There is a new—"

"I can't." Kenna stopped next to her mother's car and stared into the front seat, trying not to let the woman behind the wheel see the near-emotion on her face.

"What? Why, I don't understand, Kenna. We made these plans day before yester—"

"Yes, I know. Not tonight."

The dome light came on when Allison opened the car door and clamored out of her seat. She touched Kenna's arm as if to stop her from going back toward the truck but there was no need. Kenna was frozen where she stood, fixated on the back seat of her mother's car.

Next to a pile of magazines was one of Kenna's old sweaters and peeking out from underneath it was a well-worn book cover.

Leaves of Grass.

She slowly opened the back door and retrieved the cover as she pulled the book from her hip pocket. It was a perfect match.

Allison paled. "What are you do—?"

The next piece of the puzzle fit itself into place. Kenna turned toward her mother and whispered through clenched teeth, "Where's Sheila?"

Before her mother could stop herself she spit, "Don't you mean Brit?"

Kenna knew in her heart that those would be the last words her mother ever spoke. She found Allison's eyes in the dim light and held them captive.

"I know where Brit is, Allison. And I know you must've made a short trip to Chicago after Sheila disappeared. Right? Mom?" Kenna continued to scream, "Right? Huh? Allison? Right? Mom?" while she moved toward the back of her truck.

As her mother turned to run, Kenna clutched the spade in her powerful hands, swung it toward Allison's head, and shattered her brain stem with a single blow. The fireflies twinkled in silence for a moment before the crickets resumed their singing.

Shovel in hand, she blinked toward the sky and followed a shooting star along its intended path. Then, for the second time that day, Kenna dug a grave with no story for the deceased. She worked from memory and by the familiar feel of the earth. There was no light to shed on the grave or the past intentions of its inhabitant. It was then that Kenna realized she knew too much—that she didn't need or want to know one more thing; not anything at all.

She cleaned her tool and placed it carefully in the back of her truck. She observed the two mounds of dirt that now stood in the moonlight and tapped her watch to the night sounds of summer. It was 11:36 p.m. when Kenna heard the train whistle off in the distance.

She slipped the watch from her wrist and took the book along with its cover out of her back pocket. After shoveling a few spades of dirt out of the center of Brit's grave, Kenna placed the book into the earth and covered it gently. She dropped her watch on Allison's mounded plot and stepped on it, grinding it into the softness until it was buried as well.

She then stepped past the sites and toward the tracks as the sound of the train grew nearer. Her chest began to rumble with the motion of the approaching train as she stepped out of the darkness and into its path.

Magellan

The present that I got for Christmas one year was a collection of life gifts that was given to me by a very unlikely soul. I do not know how it came to be that I was chosen to receive such wealth but I have not ever forgotten the preciousness of the gesture, its timeliness, or the look of the man who presented it to me. However, to understand the magnitude of the gifts I received, you might first want to understand me.

I might be described as an independent and rather depressive thinker. When caught in the confines of my own mental wheel of destruction, I frequently spin into a fierce and cynical melee that causes much distance between me and those few who have sought my presence. Outwardly, it would appear that I have isolated myself quite comfortably from all who choose to live. In fact, however, my tortured and solitary existence had led me to the only reasonable solution that I could conclude.

As I prepared to turn on the gas oven, I checked the duct tape seal around each window to ensure its tightness. After years of pretending to be unfeeling, disconnected, and bemused, my life had dwindled to a short note on my kitchen table that voiced nothing more than the obvious, "It is time for me to move past the confines of hopelessness. Do not resuscitate." I could not bring myself to write my truest thoughts onto the paper. Ironically, this was the fact which most likely brought me to my personal point of desperation.

I made my way through the apartment to be certain that all things were in order before I went to lay my head in the black mouth of the stove. The television softly prattled about nothing I can recall until I heard the words "Avenue H." I momentarily stopped my wandering and padded toward the set in search of the remote. The sight of my past on the TV in my living room made me smile ever so slightly.

In the middle of a cold blast from the north, Chicago streets can buckle under the pressure of the ice and snow, causing sinkholes and road craters the size of a city bus. Although I had not seen these holes first-hand, there were entire news segments dedicated to the phenomenon, complete with pictures of cars sticking precariously out of the fissures and reporters teetering on their edges. It was inevitable that, at some point during the interview, the camera would pan the crowd and several people of questionable sanity would wave and say hello to their mothers while pointing to the hole in the ground as if to say, "Wow, will you look at that?"

It was this particular news story that caught my attention and made me forget for a moment my Christmas Eve mission. There was a certain sinkhole reportedly at Avenue H on the south side where I had lived as a child. It was on Avenue H that my father had died peacefully in his bed after sixty years of living there. A year later, my mother sat in my father's favorite chair and, with no warning to the rest of us, went off to meet him, her heart no longer breaking. Every memory of my childhood angst that I could muster came from the vicinity of that house, its backyard and alleyway full of my indelible youth.

On this snowy December evening, the news reporter and the questionable people waving at the camera were standing directly in front of the cookie-cutter house where I had negotiated and finally traded my young years for a professional career and a downtown apartment. I had thought little of our home on Avenue H since my sister, Lisa, and I had buried our mother twenty-five years ago. Now Lisa owns a string of coffee shops in Tacoma and seldom calls to check in but that is another story altogether. Suffice it to say, that was another of my life's failings.

I glanced at the clock, ticking toward midnight, and tried to shake off the newscast but the sight of my old house and the gaping hole in front of it made me curious. While I weighed the decision about whether to go out into the night or turn on the oven, an odd sound came from directly over my left shoulder and startled me. I snapped round to confront the noise and was surprised that there was absolutely nothing there. The noise began again, this time from my right, and sounded like a word, or words, being spoken, "Cometow-herlovanhopabid, Discoallyoevrnednsid."

"Maybe I am going crazy," I thought. "How ironic! Let's see . . . be crazy? Or dead? Crazy? Dead?"

I chose crazy, at least, for the moment and threw on several layers of clothing, bracing myself as the voice and words now came from my left and my right. It came from the telephone in its cradle and a camera on the desk; it echoed from the picture of the Grand Canyon on my wall and a half-dead plant near the front door. I had a sudden and overwhelming urge to see that sinkhole so I grabbed my coat and hat as I sailed out the door and on to the street.

"I can die later," I reasoned.

I kept concentrating on the voice, trying to understand. "Come-to . . . tow? Come to! What? Come to what?"

I hailed a cab and pulled the hood of the parka in closer to my face as I gave the cabbie my childhood address. The head rest in the cab began to chant the gibberish that I had just left in my apartment where I had been about to off myself and I had no idea why it was so important for me to see a sinkhole during sub-zero weather in the middle of the night. Aside from that, Christmas was going relatively well.

Rolling past the Sears Tower, the streets white as milk from salt and snow, I closed my eyes to try and make sense of the words from the voice. "Come to . . . whalo? Whee lov? Where lo . . . ?" I struggled out loud with the syllables until the cabbie stared hard at me in the mirror with a look that asked, "Do-I-need-to-call-the-cops? Do-you-have-a-gun? Are-you-nuts?" I glanced toward his picture and thought I should give him the keys to my apartment so he could use the gas oven.

My watch read 12:30 a.m. when the cab rolled to a stop in front of my old house. The icy winds leveled off to a stalwart breeze as I stepped out and onto Avenue H. The scene appeared slightly eerie to my senses. While I had changed, not so much as a crack in the sidewalk had been altered on my childhood street. The voice had stopped and the sounds of my father calling Lisa and me in for supper echoed in my head as I instinctively looked toward the stoop where I had seen him stand so many times. So lost I was in these memories, I had not noticed a slight, elderly man with usually large hands standing almost directly to my left side.

"That's a very big hole, isn't it?"

I shrieked so loud that the echo bounced off of the tiny houses down the avenue and into the next block.

"Sorry," he chuckled, "I have a knack for doing that to people—without meaning to, of course. Glad to see that you got my message." As he spoke, his eyes never left the hole in the street and I realized that I knew him somehow. His profile, his voice, even his stance were all familiar to me as I tried to place him from the list of people I had known. Definitely not a relative. Old school teacher, maybe? Neighbor, perhaps.

"Message? What message?" I asked. "I don't mean to be rude, sir, but do I know you?"

His eyes twinkled as he continued to stare into the hole. "You might know me. In fact, if you think you do then you quite possibly do, don't you think?"

"Well, what might your name be, sir?"

"Oh, I have several names, mostly from the first and second millenniums of my infinite lifetimes, although throughout the universe most recently—" He stopped abruptly when he saw the look of skepticism on my face.

"Uh, what? . . . I . . . uh . . ." It struck me that while I was having this breakdown of sorts, I was also on a deserted street with a bona fide crazy person and I tried to put some distance between the old man and myself.

Reading my mind, he said, "Easy there, Magellan, I'm not crazy but I can see how you might think so."

"Magellan?" I asked. "Who's Magellan?"

He answered, "Why, you, of course."

Then he proceeded to push me into the large, black sinkhole.

Tumbling, I realized, was an odd and exhilarating motion. It was startling, yes, but I found myself, surprisingly, without fear or hesitation. "What spell is this?" was the question in my brain but my body was light and billowy as feathers and, soon enough, I did not care to question any longer. I might've fallen for an hour or a mere split of a second. I do not know or care since I have learned that how long it takes to get where you are going is not important.

The old man's huge hand on my shoulder brought me to a gentle stop as I landed upright in the most wondrous of places I had ever seen. There were countless suns and moons that hung in a vast, aqua blue sky over my head and a brilliant silver lake just steps away. It was an enormous relief, somehow, to be in this haven and I was about to say so to my companion. As I took breath to speak, I recognized the intake of air into my lungs as a precious and rare experience. Tears fell silently from my eyes and face as I simply breathed from this unfettered space of seemingly endless time. "This is it!" I reasoned. "This is eternity and I am in it."

The old fellow looked toward my heart and read my ecstasy. "No, this is not eternity, Magellan, but it is an eternal place."

"Then where am I, sir?" I begged. "And please, tell me who you are."

His brow furrowed across his wide forehead before he spoke. "There are enough answers in your head already, my friend. Let your tears teach you that you do not need more than you already have."

"May I at least have a name to call you, sir?"

"Yes, you may."

"And what might that be?"

He momentarily brought a crooked forefinger to his pointed nose and then suddenly declared, "Harrington Olivier Pixley, Esquire, at your service."

"Or maybe 'sir' is sufficient," I muttered.

"As you wish, Magellan."

I gazed round again, rubbing my eyes, and thought about how strange and stellar any particular moment of life could be. I did not notice whether or not I was dreaming but believed all that I saw and experienced to be as real as the story I am telling you. I was living a perfectly amazing instance and, although I am not a religious person, I felt my own dormant faith stir. This odd little fellow had to be an aberration or perhaps a small psychotic break from working too hard but I felt tender and ridiculously happy. Quite strange for me and not at all what one might expect to feel while breaking down from over-work or near suicide. Moreover, I was the world's foremost cynic and resident sourpuss; still here I was, giving this situation my acute and undivided attention. To me, if that is not faith, I don't know what is.

I decided not to give any voice to my own mental bantering and simply stated, "I will call you Henry. Is that all right, sir?"

"What you call me is not important, child. That you remember me is what will matter," he replied.

I eyed my companion steadily. "You are quite strange, Henry. Decidedly peculiar and yet, I don't seem to mind at all. Why is that? And I am in this wonderful place at the bottom of a city sinkhole instead of at home with my head in the oven. How is that possible? And what do you mean that I should remember you? Why should I?"

Henry raised a hand in surrender. "My, my, friend, you are a talking head, are you not? Breathe, if you can, and enjoy these few moments. They pass so quickly, such moments as these."

As he uttered the last word from his mouth, he blew a kiss toward the heavens and the once-austere blue sky exploded into shimmering emerald green. Shooting stars fell luxuriously around and into the placid lake while the suns and moons swayed gently in perfect time. I was mesmerized and humbled by the wonder of the sight and once again implored my companion.

"I must know where this place is, Henry. I feel as if I have been here before but I am seeing it for the first time. Can that be?"

"If you say it is so, Magellan, then it is so."

"You are not really much help are you, Henry?"

"Oh, I am as much help as you ask for, Magellan."

"Now look . . ." I started.

Henry chuckled in a most annoying manner and clasped his huge right hand behind my neck firmly. He held me still and, with the thumb of his left hand, began to rub the spot in between my eyebrows. He stared intensely at nothing I could see and continued to circle my forehead with his thumb.

"Keep your eyes open and don't furrow your brow." He grunted and carried on with the motion.

Slowly at first, then more quickly, a vision came to me that I realized to be a gift. I was standing in an enormous crowd of people of every possible race and creed. Hands entwined, we were quiet enough to feel a collective beat, steady and true, that moved through each of us and on to the next. Together then apart, we felt all of life pulsating, piercing our very existence and, while I could see the differences in each person present, I knew somehow that we were all exactly the same. It was peace; it was the presence of all who choose to listen as the eternal heart beats.

Henry abruptly stopped the circular movement on my head and looked deeply into my eyes.

"Can you see what is right in front of you, Magellan?"

"I did see, Henry, I did, but it is gone now. Who were those people? How extraordinary that I was perfectly content in their presence, don't you think?"

"Well, not really so surprising, eh? You like people, don't you?"

I paused and scrupulously contemplated the question. Did I like people? "Sure, well, yes, I think, I . . . maybe . . . I guess I don't really know the answer to that."

"Good for you. Perfect answer. You are a brilliant adventurer, friend. Ha, ha! I knew you would begin to come round—"

"What in the name of all that's holy are you talking about, sir?" My query seemed only to cause his smile to explode further.

"You answered a question without asking one in return. That is a monumental step for you, Magellan."

I mentioned that he was an odd fellow, yes?

Henry placed his left hand over my heart and right hand between my shoulder blades, tightly holding me together. "Quickly!" he exclaimed. "There is little time to waste."

The little man's breath smelled strangely like sweet clover as he squeezed me firmly, front to back. Through his hand, the heart in my chest began to ache with an agony that quickly swelled into a rapturous joy. I can tell you that this heart of mine surely broke into countless pieces only to reappear stronger and kinder than my heart had ever been and it all happened in a matter of mere moments. My witness to this exquisite transformation was beginning to look haggard and drawn but the twinkle was abundant in his ageless eyes. Henry removed his hands from me and I quickly righted my body before almost collapsing into him. My balance seemed precarious and I weakened as my companion stepped away from me to catch his breath. Again, he blew a kiss toward the heavens and the sky became a magnificent rainbow of color with beautiful trees and fields of wildflowers on my left and right as far as I could see. The silence and serenity of the vision was breathtaking.

"Beautiful, isn't it, Magellan?"

"I have never seen such quiet beauty, Henry." My eyes drank in the surroundings, thirsty from years of damaged memories and unfortunate sights. There was nothing in my vision that could not be embraced and loved and I understood this to be a gift as well. With my heart wide open, I could see what was truly beautiful in the world; those people and this place, the heartbreak and that joy; all together, it was what we chose to see, think, and feel that determined how beautiful we allowed the world to be.

Henry was intensely studying my face, in particularly my mouth, when I finally realized his attentions.

"What?" I asked. "What is it?"

"You're ready! Come over here," he said, kneeling down onto the rich and downy grass, "and kneel, facing me directly."

I was embarrassed at the thought of it and he must've reckoned so because he then said, "Time is too short to allow discomforts between people, Magellan. When you are properly filled, you will understand."

I sank onto my knees in front of Henry and, studying his eyes, suddenly realized that he and I had known each other all of my life. He was my present and my future. He embraced my shortcomings, my triumphs, my losses, my humanity; he was the breath blown into me, my only savior and my answer without question. Henry was my own near-death come to life.

Harrington Oliver Pixley Esquire was my HOPE.

Before I could speak, Henry wrapped his arms tightly around my neck and began to speak in my ear.

"Listen carefully to what you've heard, Magellan, for what comes next can only come from you. Bury your head into my shoulder, quickly, and hang on! Hear again what the voice that brought you here is saying."

I felt a rush of adrenaline spirit through me as Henry whispered in my ear the now familiar sounds of the words I had heard. "Cometow-herlovanhopabid, discoallyoevrnednsid."

"I don't understand, Henry. I've tried and I make no sense of it."

"Don't try, Magellan. Breathe. And listen. Your head is in the way. Close your eyes, friend, and feel the words move into you. Take them into your belly and store them in your muscles and bones. The meaning will take its proper place if you simply trust."

Again, he whispered and, this time, I breathed. The deeper my breath, the more memory I had of the gifts I'd received; the countless people entwined and listening to the rhythm of life, the breaking and healing of my own fractured heart, and the beauty and wonder in the silence of nature. Slowly at first, and then more quickly, the sounds of Henry soaked into my being; the words began to take shape out of my mouth and into my soul.

"Come to . . . where lo . . . ve . . . love. Come to where love . . . nd . . . and ho . . . hop? Hope . . . come to where love and hope . . . abid? Abid? Abide! Come to where love and hope abide . . . dis . . . disco?"

"You are so close to finished, Magellan!" Henry's labored voice was soft and weak. "You will soon have all you need, friend. I am fading but you will not forget ever again, I promise."

"I finally know you, Henry, and I do not want to live without you."

"You won't, Magellan, you won't. Discoallyoevrnednsid . . ." he encouraged.

"Okay, disco . . . discob . . . discov . . . discover! Discover ally . . . discover all yo . . . discover all you? Discover all you'll ev . . . ever! Discover all you'll ever ned . . . need . . . Discover all you'll ever need insid . . . inside! Discover all you'll ever need inside! Come to where love and hope abide and discover all you ever need inside!"

With the last word out of my mouth, the frigid Chicago wind brought me back into the present. On my knees at the edge of the sinkhole, eyes tightly shut, and hugging my own torso intensely, I felt the icy winds of the city whip around my parka. My knees were cold from kneeling on the concrete and the sinkhole in front of me was simply that: a big, black hole. I glanced at my watch and, smiling, could only shake my head. It was 12:31 a.m., sixty seconds after I had stepped out of the cab.

It is true that what happens in a mere moment can replace the misfortunes of a lifetime.

I stood up and quickly glanced all round looking for Henry but the street seemed dark and lifeless. I breathed deeply and thought of all the beautiful gifts in this world that Henry had given to me. To think that I had almost missed receiving them. It was only a few hours ago that I was ready to quit living and now, well, now the city and its people were wonderful; my life was peaceful, and I was content. I turned my grinning face to go and Henry's words came to me again. "Come to where love and hope abide and discover all you need inside."

He was right. I understood.

As long as I can offer love and hold onto hope, then all that I truly need is inside, in this tattered and tender heart of mine. The relief of his words and the fullness of finally knowing how tender and precious each breath of life was made my eyes sting and I fought back the tears, just a little. I didn't want to get too sentimental from the experience. I am a Midwesterner, after all.

I heard a car approaching and turned just in time to see the cab drop its backseat passenger directly in front of the big, black hole in the street. As the cab headed toward me, I flagged it down and I lowered my head to step into it. From the corner of my eye, a slight, elderly man with unusually large hands suddenly appeared beside the person who was staring intently into the sinkhole.

"That's a very big hole, isn't it?"

Tummies

On June 16th, 1997, Ona Braden was startled into wakefulness by a reasonless dream.

4:15 a.m.

The silence in her house contrasted the disquieting pounding in her heaving chest.

Outwardly listening for any unusual sound, she placed her sweating hand between her breasts and inwardly counted the awkward beats of her racing heart.

112 beats per minute.

She pushed herself up from the right side of the queen-sized pillow top and glanced to her left, as if there would be someone there to comfort her. It was an old and wishful thought-turned-habit that forced her to briefly seek solace on the opposite side of her bed; one that shamed her and, yet, returned like a poet in the night to seduce her once again.

There's cake.

Ona stood. This feat of rising was seriously precarious in the early stages of her consciousness but she managed to maneuver through the narrowness by leaning from dresser to bed until she safely arrived at the bedroom door. Once there, she turned left, toward the kitchen, but quickly reversed her decision—

No cake, fat ass. Not now.

—and moved right, into the bathroom—

Let's get started since you're awake.

—to begin the unspeakable rituals of her life.

Get moving or you won't have time.

Standing in the dark—

Breathe, blow, breathe, blow.

—she could almost feel angelic beauty slip into her eyes and hair and toothy grin. She imagined that the body in the bed could see her white teeth from the empty room. "Someone always admires me in the dark," she thought. "I am never alone in the black of night."

Ona meant to turn on the light at that very moment but it seemed too early somehow and her eyes began to water and burn. If only she could stay here, pitched into black, for maybe an hour or even a day—

Crybaby, bitch.

—then the light and the sun could not destroy the loveliness in her eyes and hair and smile. Enormous tears rolled silently down the sides of her face and vanished into the creases of skin that hugged her neck. She sighed, then breathed. Then sighed again. It was the light that made Ona cry; its harshness and truth forced the day to begin—with or without her, it always began—bringing impossible odds and no small sliver of shame.

You should be ashamed, pig. Turn on the light. Look at yourself.

She placed her hands on the sink and leaned into the blackness for the last time of the day. Ona glanced toward the bedroom and thought of its emptiness; the bed sheets now cold and desperate for cover. She knew she should turn on the light. Just flip the switch and get on with it. Still her doughy fingers gripped steadfast to the porcelain fixture and drummed a rolling cadence while the tears continued to flow into the bowl below.

The cake was creating havoc. She thought about calling in sick—

What is wrong with you, Stupidass? You can't afford another day off, you whiny puke! Turn on the light and look at your pathetic self.

—but knew that her boss would dock her pay for another missed day. No sick, no vacation. No time.

Ona reared her head back, let go of the sink, and leaned against the wall behind her. She wiped her face and eyes with the front of her flannel nightgown and squeezed snot from the ends of her nostrils, letting it drip from her fingers on to the floor. "I'm ready now. I can start," she whispered.

Stand up straight. You'll never get that sack off if you don't stand up.

The floor creaked as she pushed herself off the wall and into a standing pose. She balled the nightgown from the waist into her fists until her knees, hips, and finally, her stomach were all exposed to the dark. Now came the difficult part. She turned toward the door, bent forward, and began to pull the flannel shift upward toward her head. Inch by inch, Ona struggled to pull the heavy garment over her head; hands tugging, twisting, around, underneath—

You tub of lard, you can't even get your fat sack off.

—until finally it fell on to the floor, covering the snot she had dropped.

Two birds with one stone.

She put her foot on the gown and, in one brief breath, wiped from the floor the memory of her tears. She kicked the garment into the hall, turned toward the mirror, and reached for the light switch. Eyes shut tight, she turned on the light.

She hesitated. "Maybe if I squint, it will not happen," she reasoned. She squeezed her cheeks muscles until her eyes were tiny slits of blue hidden deep among the long lashes.

Come on, you heifer.

"I am trying to do this right . . . objectively . . . like a normal person."

You are—

"Crazy." Pause. "I know."

Chickenshit.

Ona knew that if she spoke out loud again, the battle would rage forever and she would be late for work. She took a deep breath and imagined that she held a small and captive bird in her hands. Tenderly squeezing her imaginary pet, she sporadically fluttered her eyes open and focused on her face in the mirror. The pale and puffy skin stealthily oozed into her conscious creating yet another unspeakable memory. She took her eyes from her face and perused the enormous body to which she was attached.

There! That's it! Take a good look at the fruits of your labor, you putrid fucking oaf, you make me sick!

It happened every morning inside her quiet house, just out of her lonely bed, that Ona Braden faced the shameful result of her not-so-hidden image in the glass. She saw her obese and stinking torso with its gigantic appendages hanging irreverently on her tortured and burdened bones; her wounded skin still oozing from the previous morning's ritual like a milky red river running through mountains of flesh. She saw, with nocuous comfort, the huge fists of belly fat that she had hash-marked in at least a hundred places with a small pair of sharp scissors she kept in the medicine chest. Her thighs, inside and out, were also marked with the familiar, short bursts of cut skin and, in some places, muscle. In the pits of her arms and on the sides of her torso were the same intimate patterns of scissored annihilations.

Feel better now, Baby?

Actually, she did.

The external transformation would've been slight to the casual observer but, internally, it was cathartic for Ona. She stared directly into the center of the mirror, fixated on the enormous complexity of the mutilation, and saw something strange and hopeful; something beautifully unspeakable. In front of the glass, the practiced attempts for excellence on her arms and legs faded from sight and she focused on the only truth she had ever fully understood, the scissored slits on her stomach. As she gazed into the mirror, she admired the handiness and skill of her efforts. The precision and perfection of the skin slices were impressive. Each one measured exactly two inches and presented at a flawless, perpendicular angle from her straightest standing position. The Tummies, as she affectionately called them, were the guardians of her humanity; the gatekeepers of her weightiness. Without them, she would die of loneliness or some other quiet tragedy, she was sure of it.

The silence in Ona's head went unnoticed for those few moments of peace as she reacquainted herself with the Tummies. Then she remembered, and the peace, the perfection, was shattered.

Do you really think that I don't see your ridiculous attempts to piss me off? Think you can forget me, you cow? Your Tummies are your weakness, you fucking rag. Long after they are gone, I will be here, pulling your sorry ass out of the bathroom and onto the bus. You're late. Stop staring at your fat gut and get the stuff.

Ona stole one last look at her reflection in the mirror and then turned to the medicine chest. She hesitated ever so slightly before she opened the cabinet door and reached for the scissors—

Left hand, left hand only! Can you remember that, Stupid?

—careful to avoid any visual or physical contact with her right hand. The right hand must never know—

Set them on the right side of the sink today.

—what the left hand is doing.

She placed the scissors on the right side of the sink.

Are they even?

Even.

Are you sure?

The interior of Ona's torso began to churn with a familiar uneasiness. Something wasn't right. She began to panic, studying the scissors for the error in placement. What was it? What wa—

You cannot get the simplest rule straight, can you, fat girl? Move . . . the . . . cutters . . . to the edge where they belong!

First, she fisted her right hand behind her back to stop it from helping its left mate. Then, she quickly moved the scissors to the edge of the sink and checked them a second and then a third time to be certain that they were directly parallel to the sink's right side.

Now that's *even.*

A delicate signal of acceptance stole into her conscious and she flushed with tentative relief.

Breathe while you can.

"That scares me—"

Then why *do you say it?*

All of the earth as she knew it stood still while the seconds ticked away inside of her tiny bathroom. She knew that trouble was closer than usual because of the cake. She had to be perfect this morning—perfect as the Tummies—or she would not be allowed to breathe for the day.

You are a waste of oxygen.

When she made mistakes in the morning, Ona repented by not allowing herself a full breath from the time she left her house for work until the time she got home, ten hours later. She only allowed herself to take short, shallow pants of air and she had fainted on more than one occasion from the discipline.

"I can do this," she thought. "I can . . ."

Suddenly and without warning, anger overtook her fragile sensibilities and she jerked forward—

What are you doing?

—confronting herself in the mirror—

This is not what we do.

—and grabbing the sides of her massive face and fleshy neck.

You and your—

She squeezed the folds of skin tight in her hands and her black thoughts began to spill into a vocal tirade. "—fat, fat, fat face! God, I hate you. You disgust me. Weak and lazy, dumb, stupid, ass with a fucking balloon for a face—"

Stop it this insta—

"Shut up!" Again she realized it was the cake that was causing this insubordination. The cake had to go.

She shook the doughy tissue beneath her fingers with a violence that would surely bruise her for a month and gouged the pockmarks of her neck skin with her nails. "Who in God's name would even look at you? Go get another fat piece of food and shove it in your freaky fat face." Ona stomped into her unlit kitchen and looked blindly around each counter top until she eyed the tin of cake. Seething and muttering,

"You want to eat, huh? Here, let's shove some more garbage into you, you cow."

She unleashed her hands from her face, knocked the tin cover onto the floor and buried her fingers into the center of the moist dessert. The letters HAPPY BIRTHDAY O! were written in cheery yellow icing between the thin slices cut from the edges by her co-workers. "Take it home", they had insisted, "bring the tin back later." Those well-meaning co-workers had no idea what they had done.

She slapped her cake-filled hands onto her face and shoved mounds of cake into her mouth. "Mmmmm," she shrilled sarcastically, "good for you! Come on, you can fit more in, can't you?" Again and again, until there was nothing left, Ona Braden angrily stuffed the cake into her mouth and hated herself more with each swallow. Tears flowed down her face and the salty taste mingled with the sweetness. Her hair and eyelashes were caked with icing and the floor of the kitchen was covered with the remnants of her tirade. Puffing and spent, she blinked. Then she blinked again.

Slowly, the reality of what she had done crept into her thinking process and she trembled.

Get down on the floor you spineless bubble-ass bitch.

Ona fell to her knees and her battered nakedness fractured the inky air surrounding her.

Pay penance.

"I—"

You know how this works. Face down on your fat gut and feed like the swine you are.

She paused.

Pause? What . . . fucking . . . pause?

She hesitated to finish her descent onto the floor. She visualized her Tummies being concealed by the dark mess in front of her thighs and the image made her sick.

What is wrong with you? Get with the program . . . Now!

She glanced toward the window above the sink as the earliest morning light crept into the room. Outside, hidden in the grass, spring crickets hummed a monotonous dirge that signaled their forlorn embrace of the ill-fated summer to come.

"I can't."

Can't? No, no, no! This is not acceptable! On the floor, fat bitch! You are in serious, serious trouble. Your right hand is exposed, you are in the kitchen, and you have eaten! Your precious Tummies will not save you from this breach of etiquette, Dimwit ass. You need discipline and I . . . I . . . I will see that you get it. Now, get down on the tiles and worship that fat shit. Those Tummies are insidious and they need to be concealed by your shame on the floor. God, how stupid can you be?

Ona's stomach repelled the sugary offering that she had so rage-fully consumed and almost immediately she started to heave its contents onto the already-hideous floor. She shook violently as, again and again, her body rejected the massive quantity of cake she had ingested. On hands and knees, in the midst of her regurgitation, Ona Braden caught sight of her precious Tummies in the breaking light of day; each flawless mark of her beast, like dead soldiers, lay side by side in precise slumber. It occurred to her that their blatant isolation from one another directly matched her loneliness somehow and it was then, in that awareness, that she began to fight against any hope. Still trembling, she placed both hands on either side of the vomit on the floor and began the slow process of standing on her feet.

Where do you think we are going?

The light in the kitchen was an ominous gray milk, hanging and dank. As she crawled toward the counter for balance, Ona remembered a story she had read about a twelve-year-old girl who was raped by her father while her mother comforted her by holding the girl's head in her lap. She had memorized the story and wept for weeks in the bathroom stalls at work each time she visualized the helplessness and inevitable shattering of a life barely formed. Tears sprung to her eyes as she now thought of the young girl again.

Oh, come on! Not that tired fucking story again.

She pulled herself into a standing position and surveyed the indelible evidence of her truth left on the floor. She knew now that these atrocities, not the Tummies, were her most honest offerings and that thought alone sent stealth shivers into her being. Her precision skill with scissors could no longer fend off the inevitable awareness that the life she was given had been petrified by pain. Her Tummies were only the physical sign of her brokenness and would surely leave her, unless—

Unless?

—unless she could somehow overcome the now dreadful truth about her existence. She leaned into the counter and dropped her head to eye the Tummies once again.

"What do you think, Tummies? What should we do to rectify?"

Who are you talking to?

Pause.

Ona braced her body forward against the cabinets and, with the full force of an experienced hammer hitting a nail, rammed her head into the granite counter in front of her. Thin, black blood first trickled, then pulsated out of the center of her skull as she stood, panting and grasping at her thoughts.

"Shut up! I am sick to *death* of you! Shut up for both of our sakes, will you? Just shut up, shut up, shut up—I cannot think with you spitting and spewing from the mouth *all of the time*. No more voices . . ."

She stood silent and waited for the anger of her stupidity to overtake her but it never came. She welcomed the pain from her head like a mother would celebrate a suckling child. Blood now covered most of the surface in front of her and had begun to drip down the sides of the cabinet. Ona felt feathery and softly kissed as the new memory nestled into her brain. In the back yard, a cardinal sang and the wind carried its distant song until the sound was nothing more than a whisper.

Think/breath, think/blow—

The room spun and then miraculously righted itself. For an instant, her heart leapt with the promise of the rapturous end of the world when heaven's saints would honor her bountiful body and the Tummies with a defining embrace.

"I am the quick and the dead," she said.

From the bathroom she heard the faintest vibration, deep and low; her name called out into the air around the corner. She trailed a ribbon of blood as she retraced her steps from a few precious moments ago and crept toward the sealing of her fate. Rounding the doorway into the bathroom, Ona saw the slightest bit of light on the scissors and it gave her courage to begin the process of redemption. She hesitated only slightly before sliding her fingers into the Tummies' shears and slipping down the wall to sit on the bathroom floor.

Silence.

She carefully examined each side of the steel cutters and caught a glimpse of her matted and bloody hair in their blade. The large split in her forehead was an imperfect crack in her skull and her face was covered with blood, tears, and cake. She put the tip of the scissors into her mouth and tasted the metal against her lips. Turning the scissors to the left, she slipped her tongue between the blades and, with her thumb and forefinger, bared down slightly. She tasted the salty blood as she shut her eyes and pushed harder to close the scissors and shear her tongue free from the constraints of her mouth. Two inches of the muscle fell into her lap.

"No more voices . . . no more words," she silently reasoned, "almost free."

Ona's eyes burned from trying to see past the truth into forgiveness but exhaustion and habit are unkind companions. She studied the enormity of her body with disgust and gently fingered her beautiful Tummies while her blood ran out of her mouth and forehead onto the torso that she hated and loved.

She positioned the point of the cutters onto her right wrist and began the arduous process of clipping at the paper-thin skin until it finally burst. Her reward was the bright red blood of a vein opening onto the floor. As it pulsed its way from the constraints of her body, Ona Braden relaxed into the journey of being present and witnessed her own emancipation.

It was 5:22 a.m.

Later, when the news of her death finally reached her workplace, Ona's name was mentioned around the water cooler, whispered at lunch tables, and toasted at happy hours. Her empty desk would be stared at ominously as co-workers recalled every detail of her sketchy existence. They speculated about how such secrets could be kept from them as if they were her closest confidantes; they silently thanked God and worried about whether or not this magnitude of tragedy would strike closer to home next time.

Ona Braden was bigger than life in her last acts of desperation, remembered for the tiniest of her kind and helpful characteristics. Her puzzle of truth was never solved but, for those who found her, the jagged and haunting memory of her discovery indelibly made its mark. Burned into their mental visions, a word—"Tummies"—scrawled in blood across a tiled bathroom floor, and a vivid, ghostly image of the mutilated and rail-thin young woman who had written it there.

The Habit

There's a parish over there and down the street. It's attached to St. Michael's church on the corner and that's where it all started. For the life of me if you would've told me things were going to happen the way they did, I would've never guessed it. But, the truest part of life is the most unbelievable, that's my philosophy.

Anyway, I just love a good flower and the lilacs across the street from the church are the prettiest you ever saw. The bouquet from those bushes just makes me want to bury my face in their fragrance. And, in fact, that's what I was doing the day that Alice Weaver—tall Al we called her in school—came out of the front door of the parish, screeching like a hoot owl. At first I thought there was a fire or something like it and she was trying to get somebody's attention. The next glance told me that she was crying and hiding her tears with the blue sun-hat that she was holding on either side of her cheeks. Her face was red and she clung to the hat's brim, trying to pull it down over her swollen eyes. I wondered who might be dead because that was the only time you saw anybody crying over the age of twelve in Hollowdale. Strong stock, we are, and we don't air our laundry, clean or dirty.

Well, Alice scurried down the steps like a giant mole in a blue bonnet, clutching her purse in one hand and a hankie in the other. She pointed her nose toward the sidewalk and marched off to have her feelings, I guess. By now, of course, I was curious about what was wrong with tall Al and thought I might go inspect the parish for clues. I got all the way to the porch when Sister Michael Mary Morgan—Sister Mike they called her in church—came bounding through the door with her habit flying this way and that. Now I had seen Alice and she looked bad but Sister Mike looked even worse. Her usual stone face was crunched into a pucker with a frown that would've scared a gargoyle. She barely glanced at me as she sped by in her bolts of black linen and I watched her trail tall Al down the street. Now this occurrence may not have struck many other folks in this town as particularly odd, but me? I am exceptional in my powers of observation. I watched the nun and the mole meet up about a block down the street, right in front of my own house. From what I could see, Sister Mike and tall Al looked to be having a lover's spat. Maybe most people wouldn't have known that but, like I said, I see things that other people don't.

Sister Mike was studying her shoes and gesturing with her hands. Alice was sniffling into her hankie and rubbing the buckle on her purse like it was a worry stone. Course, I couldn't hear a thing since I was so far away but there was a cloud of something, all right. And it was hanging just over them. During a vigorous head-shaking, Sister Mike caught sight of me out of the corner of her eye and clenched her teeth toward Alice. I moved toward them at a clipper's pace so I didn't prolong their agony at having been discovered. See, I knew what they were feeling. I had managed the same kind of argument from time to time with my Deanna for over twenty-eight years until she died. There are days when I wish she were next to me, fighting about nothing that we would ever remember. Hell, I wish I were with her, for that matter.

Anyhow, the lovebirds were stuck in a thicket; I could tell that. But I wasn't quite sure just how to help them out. If I was direct about what I knew, then they would be terrified that I would blab to somebody about them. But, if I wasn't direct, then they would be falling all over themselves trying to make up excuses. And, if you ask me, excuses are a waste of precious air. Well, they were staring and buzzing at each other to shush when I finally got down the block to them in front of my house. Before either of them could say a word, I decided to speak up and say what needed to be said.

"Girls, you are wearing each other out, aren't you? Don't speak, Mike—can I call you Mike without the 'sister'?" I took her wide-mouthed silence to be a "yes." "Now, don't speak until I have had my say, all right?"

The women stood there looking at me and I'm sure they were wondering whether to run in opposite directions or just stand there and take it. Beads of sweat were collecting on Mike's upper lip and sliding down where her sideburns would've been. Alice seemed less nervous and more curious about what I might say.

"You are obviously in love, or at least, think you're in love since love is really not a proven fact but a long trail of guesses and when two peop . . . sorry. Let me start again."

I paused.

"See, after a certain amount of time, your relationship starts to be tested by almost every little thing because you realize that the other person is not quite the same as you thought that . . . nope, that's not it, either. Just give me a minute."

I stood there looking at the mannish nun and her gawking girl-friend and realized that I was going to lose them pretty quick if I didn't say something they could understand.

"I know about the two of you. There. That should be enough."

The red-faced Mike snorted and then breathed deep to draw my undivided attention so she could make her statement. I studied her five o'clock shadow and waited for her gravelly voice.

"Why, I can't imagine what in the world you are talking about, Lydia. Miss Weaver and I were discussing matters of great biblical importance when she was called to the telephone for a matter of grave importance. So important in fact that she shinnied out of the vestry so quickly that I . . ." Her voice trailed off fairly close to when she saw the incredulous look on my face.

"Mike, Mike, Mike," I began, "what say we don't start the conversation with a less-than-truthful slice of excuse pie, hmmm?" The sweating, woolen-clad, nun narrowed her round eyes at me and folded her arms in defiance. "Besides, I'm concerned you might drop over with heat stroke if you keep sucking and blowing like that. Al, aren't you worried about your girlfriend?" Alice had been silent but busy up to this point, watching her enormous nun-friend butt heads with an old high school chum over the truth about her sexuality. I came to learn later that she found the exchange between Mike and me fascinating. At that moment, however, she looked more shell-shocked than bedazzled.

"Al, honey? Can you hear me?"

"Wha—? Oh, yes, Lydia, I am just so, so . . . stunned. Yes, stunned, that's it. You speak so very bold indeed and I am unsure about what to say." She truly looked perplexed, all right.

"Why, what in the world is there to say, Al, other than you're in some sort of love tryst with a nun and obviously over the edge about a quarrel you've had."

Sister Mike looked hard toward Alice as if to dare her to open her mouth. It seemed like Al might speak again but, seeing Mike, thought better of it. I continued.

"Now surely you both knew about Deanna and me for all of those years, didn't you? Everyone else in the free world did. I am a confidant, girls. Someone you can count on. Your secret's safe with me." Hearing those words, Alice burst into a fresh set of tears. "Great day, Alice Weaver, what in the world has got you so upset?"

I narrowed my gaze toward Sister Mike and, through slit eyes, began to think the worst.

"Sister, you have not hurt my friend in any way, have you? I am a peaceable woman but should I learn that you have done something along the way of one of those priests in that church of yours—"

Mike bristled. "Oh, good Lord, Lydia, don't be ridiculous!"

"I'm just saying that if there is something fishy going on here, I will know about it soon enough and there will be Hell to pay!"

"For God's sake, Alice, tell the woman that you have not been . . . handled . . . inappropriately."

Pause.

"Alice? Tell . . . her . . ."

Well, Al certainly wanted to say something but for the life of me, I could not figure out what it was. She just stood there, fidgeting with her hankie and shifting weight from one stick-like leg to another. She looked at me, pleading, to let her off the hook.

"Listen, I'll tell you what," I glanced around, "if you are worried someone might hear our conversation, then why don't we just go inside my house here and talk in private? I have some fresh-brewed tea and I think I can find a cookie or two. Come on, now, let's step inside."

Hearing my words, tall Al made a beeline for the door while Sister Mike tried to decide whether or not she should go inside. I stepped toward the porch and motioned for Mike to follow me. Once in the front hallway, I went to find refreshments and the couple moved into the living room. As I hurried toward the kitchen, I could hear their hushed and desperate tones to one another but couldn't catch what they were saying. It seemed awful confusing to me. Most people would be relieved. I had given these girls a safe haven and, although it might've been a tad scary, the least they could do was relax a little. After all, they were in the company of another one of their own kind! What in blue blazes was wrong with them? And what would the church do to a lesbian nun anyway? I reckoned that a girl almost had to prove she was a lesbian before she took her vows with that bunch. What else would those religious nuts do at night with the shades drawn and all that time on their hands?

Well, I poured the tea, found a few lemon bars to put on a tray, and moved toward the front room to continue the conversation. The unlikely pair sat at opposite ends of the sofa looking as if they had entered, and won, a Laurel and Hardy look-alike contest.

"Now, ladies, I mean to get to the bottom of this so one of you might as well speak up and tell me why you are both so upset."

After a moment, the silence was ear-splitting. I decided to change tactics.

"I don't mean to pry but, Alice, you're one of my oldest friends and I obviously am concerned at seeing you bawling like a calf. And, Sister Mike, I don't know you at all but you look mighty, well . . . bad, if you know what I mean. Out of sorts. Yes, that's what I mean to say."

Can poison shoot from a person's eyes? If so, Mike's aim was only slightly off and the venomous look she shot fell just short of killing me.

"I just want to offer my friendship and support to you. It's hard being in the closet and, quite frankly, I am happy to have other lesbians to—"

I stopped short because, at the word "lesbian," Al gasped and clasped her hand over her mouth, almost losing the tea right out of it.

"Now, there you go again, Alice. What in the world is wrong with the word 'lesbian'? No doubt you understand the term."

Alice recovered and hurriedly stated, "Yes, of course, and I am of the same mind, Lydia. After all of these years, I am glad to let you know it, in fact. I feel relieved but there's . . ." Tears welled up in her eyes and she could not finish her statement. Well, I thought, she finally spoke the fact that she was a lesbian, at least. That's something. But there was something else that didn't add up. What was it? I began to study Mike who truly looked stricken. Her hands on her knees and shoulders hunched around her ears, you would've sworn that there was a bird flying around the room. The pinched look on her face made her seem like she was holding her breath. Maybe she was.

"What is it, Mike? Are you worried about the church and what they will do? I told you that your secret's safe with me."

The sister drew breath to speak but Alice interjected.

"Oh, I don't think that the good Sister is worried too much about the church finding out she's a lesbian, are you, Mike?"

At those words, I realized that the tiff between these girls was not just a lover's spat. This was serious. An affair, perhaps? Maybe the sister had a wandering eye.

"Well," I offered, "can you speak up, Sister Mike? I want to be able to help the two of you get through this rough patch if I can."

Alice spoke again. "There is no rough patch, Lydia, although I am grateful for your kindness. Whatever relation the sister and I had, it no longer exists, believe me. I can tell you that there is *nothing* and will be *nothing* between us, no matter how hard the good sister tries. Enough said."

Alice seemed intent on keeping that vow and Sister Mike stared at the floor. Oddly enough, she seemed relieved that Al had stopped talking.

"Well, I can't quite put my finger on it but there is something that either one or both of you isn't saying. I am left with such an unsettled feeling about this whole incident. Alice, you *are* a lesbian, correct?"

"Yes, Lydia, I am. One-hundred and ten percent, beyond the shadow of a doubt, dyed-in-the-wool, card-carrying lover of women. Absolutely." Al stated her case so vehemently that my heart fluttered. I love a woman who speaks her mind, especially when she is so clearly decided.

"And are you in love with Sister Mike?"

"Believe me, not any more. Not since—" Mike suddenly broke out into a coughing fit, nearly throwing herself onto the floor. Alice stared hard at the hacking nun with contempt. After a moment of admiring Al's surprisingly stronger qualities, I turned my attention to Mike.

"And, Sister, you are in love with Alice?"

After a long pause and belly shaking sigh, Mike muttered through gritted teeth, "Yes."

"Well then, have you been . . . straying from the path of your intended?"

"What?" Mike asked.

"Have you been . . . are you . . . you know, toying with another's affections?"

"For God's sake, Lydia, what is it that you are asking me? Spit it out, child. I don't understand you."

"Are you fooling around?"

"No! I do not *fool* with anyone!"

"Hah!" Alice snorted.

So that *was* it. Sister Mike was a cheater! Well, Alice deserved better and I was about to say so when Sister Mike rose from the couch and said, "Lydia, please direct me to the restroom. This tea is making its presence known, if you understand me."

"Certainly, Sister. The facilities are just off to the left here." I rose and pointed to the small door just beyond the living room in the hallway. As Mike lumbered off, I thought that it would be my opportunity to speak to Alice alone. The bathroom door shut rather loudly and I immediately turned to my friend.

"Alice, you simply must tell me what has you so upset. I—"

"Well, you wouldn't believe me if I did tell you, Lyd—"

"But what makes you say so, Alice? I cannot imagine—"

"You are right, friend. You cannot imagine."

Alice's tone was so emphatic that I was momentarily startled into silence. While we sat in the quiet room, a sound came from the bathroom that was unmistakably familiar, although the memory was distant.

"Lord, Alice, that girlfriend of yours must've had to pee for the better part of the day! I have not heard anything that loud since my nephew was here. Why the last time he was . . ." I paused. "My *nephew* was here. That sound! It is the sound of . . . it's a . . . ohmygod, Alice, is . . . is . . . Sister Mike really a Brother Mike?" We looked at each other; I in astonishment and Alice in disgust. "You mean to tell me that . . . is she . . . is he . . . ?" I again fell speechless.

Alice slowly nodded her head as she clapped her bony hand across her mouth. She began to spit words as if she had swallowed a bag of feathers.

"Yes! Yes, it is true, Lydia, and I am *completely* beside myself! I have never in my life, well, you know, I have never *seen*, let alone *touched* a member of the opposite sex, if you know what I mean." She began to whisper conspiratorially. "Lydia, I was smitten with Sister Mike and have spent the last several months in her company. She . . . he . . . whatever . . . was very kind and soon our friendship had blossomed into, well, a romance of sorts. However, we had not . . . consummated—God, this is embarrassing—and I was confused as to why she . . . he . . . you know (she threw a thumb over her shoulder toward the bathroom) had not made the attempt. Well, today, standing in the vestibule, we had gotten very close, you know, physically? And, well, I leaned in so that she might kiss me and thought to myself, 'Well, that beard will have to go . . .' and as I was considering how to bring up the delicate subject of electrolysis, there seemed to be another part of her body that was calling for immediate attention."

I must've looked confused because Alice loudly whispered, "down there," pointed to her crotch, and drew the outline of a banana.

"Oh, yes, of course." I mentally declared myself permanently befuddled.

"I ran from the parish at the very moment I realized that Sister Mike had a package in her pocket and was definitively glad to see me. Oh, Lydia, what I am going to do? I am not interested in men and this . . . this . . . male person posing as a nun is now interested in me! Can men be nuns? God, what am I saying? Of course not. Great guns, Lydia, I can easily fall for the nun but I am *not* spiritual enough to disregard the, you know . . . surprise inside."

"Alice, I am so confoundedly overwhelmed that there is a peeing male nun in my bathroom at present that I can't seem to think of another thing. I woke up and went outside to smell the flowers. I didn't expect to find a boy-nun and his potential conquest on the sidewalk in front of my house, you know? You say that you did not know, is that right? Well, honey, you know now. What is it that you want?"

"Well, I don't want him!"

The bathroom door slammed open and Sister Mike made his way back into the living room. He was clearly nervous and could not keep his gaze steady on either of us.

"She told you then, Lydia?"

"Well, yes, she did, Sister Mike, and I am not exactly sure just what to do at the moment."

"Why must anything be done?" the big nun implored. "I lost my head, Alice."

"More than one," Alice muttered.

"And I really do care for you! I mean, I—"

"Do you make a habit of preying on unsuspecting lesbians, Mike?" I interjected.

"Of course not, Lydia. I have only the best intentions." He paused. "That is not to say that I have not had feelings for other women in my line of work but—"

"My stars, you're joking?" Alice retorted. "You mean that this is not the first time that you have tried to . . . seduce . . . a parishioner? How many others? How long have you been a nun?" Alice gasped suddenly with a new idea. "I'll bet you have children!"

"Alice, don't be ridiculous. I don't have any . . . well, I don't think I have—"

"That's it!" I interjected. "No more. I can't take it. You have desecrated my house, not to mention my bathroom, you, you, nun-in-wolf's-clothing, you. Alice, you will stay here and Mike or Harry or Charles or whatever your name is, you will leave. I need time to think."

Turning toward the door, the nun spoke. "Won't you come with me, Alice? We could just talk."

"Are you nuts?" She seethed.

"Don't go there," I whispered to Alice.

The screen door slammed behind Sister Mike as he trudged down the steps. He turned back toward the door to look at us and posed the question. "Will you tell anyone? Either of you?"

"God, you've got balls," I said.

"Don't I know it," Alice replied.

We stood at the door and watched the two hundred and fifty pound linen sack of flesh move down the block. How Alice or I could've ever believed *that* was a she was beyond me.

The day turned into evening and then to night while Alice and I shared a sigh of relief, made some dinner, and began to laugh at the situation. Alice was embarrassed. Who wouldn't be? But she became more candid and light-hearted as the evening progressed. I saw in her what I had seen in Deanna so many years ago and wondered why I had not noticed it earlier. It was there; that ultimate sense of well-being and comfort. No matter what happened to her, she would bounce back, find a place to chuckle at herself, and move past it all. I had loved that about Deanna and would soon enough come to love that about Alice.

Another love of my life at this age was a welcome surprise for me and a monumental event for Alice. She had never, well, you know, consummated *any* relationship, much to my complete astonishment.

"I was not as sought after as you, Lydia-Whose-Hot-Lips-Kissed-Every-Girl-In-Town."

"I cannot imagine why not, Alice-Who-Almost-Rode-A-Nun's-Pecker-In-Church."

CR⋅◈⋅ℬ

The best things in life are free. Like those lilacs in front of St. Michaels or the soft sound of Alice sleeping next to me. Then there are other things that are not exactly free but sought after, nonetheless.

Alice and I decided to have a chat with the priest, Father Simon, down the block just to see if he had a clue as to the sexual identity of his newest nun. The gist of the conversation went something like this.

"She's a what? She . . . He did what? She has a what?"

So on and so forth.

After explaining the damage that may have been done to the unspoiled Alice, Father Simon began to sweat profusely and reached for his hidden stash of communion wine. After all, the good Father had employed a man posing as a woman in a nun's habit who was attempting sexual relations with an adult lesbian virgin who had attended this church since she was four years old. Reaching for a drink seemed reasonable enough at that moment. Our conversation was short-lived and Simon agreed that it was best kept "in house," I believe was the term he used. Alice and I were agreeable, with a few conditions, of course. First, that Sister Mike would be defrocked or deflowered or whatever the term is for bouncing a nun from her sacred post. Father Simon vigorously agreed that was best. Second, that the church would obtain a list of the women Sister Mike had "counseled" and assist them in every way to recover from the incident. Simon was not too keen on this one.

"Oh no, ladies! How in the world would we ever manage to contact each lady in question? I'm afraid that this task is next to impossible and certainly imprac—"

I got up from my chair in the Father's office and walked toward the telephone. Hearing the dial tone, I began to press the key pad.

"Miss Lydia, we are in the middle of a conversation. What are you doing?"

"I am calling WFAY radio to report Sister Mike's penis, Father."

"No, no! We'll find a way to help the women, Lydia. My God, put the phone down."

Alice looked as if she might implode laughing but managed to keep her hat on. I, on the other hand, was deadly serious.

"Father, you have a predatory male nun on your staff. If you don't want that information passed in every Kroger's store and beauty parlor from here to Canada, then I suggest you do more than see if the church can help."

"Yes, yes, we will. Now, I am truly sorry for what has happened. Sis . . . well, Mike, will be leaving and is no longer goin—"

"That's not all, Father," Alice interjected.

"What's that?"

"There is something else that we would like for you to do, Simon," I said.

Father Simon was visibly pensive. "And what might that be, ladies?"

"Alice and I would like to be married."

The silence in the room was remarkable. I thought I heard a cotton ball drop.

"You're not serious," he said.

"As a nun's pecker," I replied.

"Are you suggesting that I? Me? You want *me* to perform a *lesbian* wedding service?"

"In the church," my beloved added.

"What? Are you . . . have you? I cannot even entertain the notion of such an atrocity."

"Careful, Padre," I cautioned.

"I mean no disrespect, Lydia, but how in the world can I do such a thing? It is against all that I believe."

"Well, it's really not about what *you* believe that matters, is it, Simon? It's about what Al and I believe. You are just there to officiate one of God's pairings. Now, do I go to the phone or do I take my girlfriend to buy her wedding dress?"

 round symbol

In the end, Alice and I did not push Father Simon to have a public wedding or even post our nuptials in the church bulletin. We had a simple ceremony, the three of us, on a quiet Saturday afternoon. Afterward, Alice and I drove into the city and spent a few days in a lesbian bed and breakfast and at the women's bookstore.

By the time we got home, Sister Mike was gone without a trace. There was some talk that perhaps she had become pregnant by the director of the senior housing development. That rumor kept us howling for a couple of months.

The church secretly assisted fourteen women in rebuilding their lives after their encounter with the good Sister and Father Simon went on to become a cardinal and an alcoholic.

My loving partner? Well, Alice has been consummated many times over and declares she is a better catholic for it. I've enjoyed overseeing the venture, if you know what I mean. Hell, I'm better for it and I'm not even catholic.

There are more than a few lessons I have taken from this experience but none so important as this: Stop and smell the flowers. Because you never know when you might meet the next love of your life running down the street being chased by an aroused man in a nun's habit; you just might have your lesbian wedding officiated by an alcoholic priest in a catholic church.

Baby

Rachel stirred when she heard a popping sound in her head. The last of a dream, she guessed, as a muffled thud brought her mostly aware. She heard the soft sounds of Saturday morning cartoons on the television in the other room. Eyes still closed, she smoothed the sheet between her and her lover, Tiana, as she reached to feel skin. Her head was pounding and she knew the sweat would start soon for both of them. There were disadvantages to sleeping in if you were a junkie. A late start meant that her body would begin withdrawal soon and they had finished the last tweak of powder at 2 a.m.

If I call Misty, maybe she'll have an ounce or so. She owes us after last night. Or maybe Tiana's got bubble gum today. No, she was at the methadone clinic yesterday . . .

As Rachel thought about their options for the day, the pain in her head began to take over her senses. She fingered her long, dark hair back from the side of her face and felt a lump next to ear. Seeing blood on her wet fingers made her heart skip.

What the . . . ?

She struggled to remember the night before with all of those people in their tiny apartment. It was the first of the month and the party had gone on until the money ran out. Her primary dealer, Franco, had danced out of the room with thousands of dollars. The rest stayed until they were sure the last of the dope was gone. At 2 a.m., Tiana had reached into her pocket and brought out a small bag of powder. The gesture was a peace offering, Rachel remembered.

She hit me in the head with the butt of her gun because I mainlined the last of the needle we were sharing. Damn . . .

Rachel had been hit plenty of times in the last two years. Sometimes it was by Tiana but mostly by dealers when she wouldn't sleep with them after they got her high. After she had discovered the soft and powerful touch of Tiana, she just couldn't do the "man" thing. Besides, if Tiana ever caught her with a man, there would be a trip to the hospital. She thought about it on days like today when there was no stash and no money but she rarely got that desperate. And she could be pretty creative.

Maybe T-bone will set us up some credit. Food stamps might get here today. We could sell those . . .

Tiana stirred next to her and turned slightly. Rachel noticed that the mid-morning light made her look fragile and sad. Every day since Tiana had introduced Rachel to heroin, she had awakened before Tiana, watched her sleep, and finally reached across the bed to kiss her. After that morning ritual, Rachel would go down the hall and into her four-year-old daughter's room for another kind of ritual. She would pick up her daughter and hold her tight, kissing and tickling her into a frenzy. They tried to be quiet—Tiana wasn't crazy about kids—but they almost never managed it.

I should get up and get the baby . . .

Jessica was the only great accomplishment Rachel had ever managed. When she became pregnant at seventeen, her parents insisted she give the baby up for adoption after it was born. While she loved her parents, she knew that she could never part with the infant. Her options were limited but her fear of losing her baby was greater than her fear of the unknown. Three days after Jessica was born, when Rachel was supposed to be signing the adoption papers, she took the baby instead and fled the rural Midwest town. She bought a bus ticket to the first big city and used most of the money she had saved to find the apartment and buy diapers.

I could take Jessica to the store with me to get milk. And maybe we'll pop over to Lake St. and see if Honey Girl is working yet. She might have some on her since she don't trust Gina with it at home. Maybe she'll front us for a few days.

Drops of perspiration formed on Rachel's upper lip and her arms felt clammy. The twitch in her hands and legs would come next. She opened her eyes again and looked around the room for signs of possibilities.

Wonder if there is any of that tequila left. That would hold it off for a few hours . . .

The bedroom was a wreck. There were pizza boxes and food wrappers all around the bed. The sagging curtains on the window were ripped and the floor, what could be seen of it, was filthy. Every kind of clothing was scattered onto the bed, chair, and floor as well.

The baby's toys were spread around and the smell of urine and feces permeated the room.

I gotta get diapers before the carpet gets ruined again . . .

Rachel leaned into her lover and kissed the top of her head before rolling toward her own side of the bed. She found the phone lying next to the nightstand in a pool of what smelled like beer. She picked it up and squeezed her eyes shut to clear her head before she made the call.

Time to play the game . . .

Blowing out a deep breath, she dialed the seven numbers and waited for her dealer to answer the phone. When she spoke, she barely recognized the dicey street dialect that fell out of her mouth.

"Franco. Yo, boy, where you at?"

"Down by da sea, lil girl, down by da sea. You up?"

"No thanks ta you, Cuz-zzzz."

"I don't call da play, baby. You grown. You know whut time bring."

"You carryin' wid you, Franco?"

Pause.

"Who wanna know? You? You gotta whole lotta shakin' goin' on?"

"Don't mess, man. You know whut we need. She ain't even up yet. I wanna get it togetha before she up."

"An' whut you doin' fer me, lil girl?"

"Whut you askin', man?"

"I ain't askin'. I wanna know whut you doin' fer the man who fix you, baby. What you got?"

"I ain't got nuthin'. My credit good, you know, it is."

"Well, you might have sumpin' I want."

Pause.

"Franco, you know I don—"

"Naw, I ain't lookin fer dat. Plenty o' dat anywhere, lil girl."

"Whut then?"

"I saw Ti had a gun wid her las' night."

"Yeah, so?"

"I take dat fer two days worth."

"I dunno nuthin' 'bout her shit, man. I cain't git involved in no gun shit."

"Den wake 'er up and tell 'er whut's on."

"I ain't doin' that, Smack! She be feelin' my head wid dat damn gun agin."

"Is on you, lil girl. You know da terms."

"I call you back, man."

Rachel trembled as she dropped the phone to the side of the bed and eyed her lover for signs of waking up. She could see beads of sweat rolling down the woman's neck and onto the sheet. Tiana moaned as her legs jerked and scissored across the mattress.

Damn, what am I gonna do? If I get up and find the gun, I could meet Franco and get the horse before she gets too twitchy. When I get home, I could convince her that somebody else musta taken the gun last night. Franco won't say nothin if I ask him not to. I'd have to take the baby with me, though. If Tiana wakes up and I'm not here, Jessica will catch hell.

Getting out of bed was not always easy. Heroin, like any other drug, might seem like a good idea while going into the body but not while leaving it. Rachel swung herself into a sitting position on the side of the bed as aching pains shot up her legs and down her arms. The quiver in her head and hands made it difficult for her to stand. She dropped to her knees, faced the bed, and used it to push herself up. Her stomach rolled and she tried to remember when she last ate anything.

Monday? Tuesday, maybe . . .

Shaking, she fell into the dresser as she slipped into a pair of jeans. The clock rocked back and forth and she reached out her hand to stop it.

10:30 a.m . . .

Tiana began to twist and turn from side to side and Rachel knew that she had to go before the woman was fully awake. She remembered the sounds of cartoons and knew that Jessica would be in front of the television. She decided to get her dressed while she called Franco back so they could get out before Tiana called to her. She pressed the redial button on the phone as she struggled into her shirt and headed toward the living room. Phone in hand, stumbling down the hall, buttoning her shirt, shaking, sweating, Rachel smiled at the thought of her daughter snuggled in a blanket, laughing at the television.

Such a sweetheart . . .

In the living room, the sound of the television seemed surreal. For just a minute, Rachel thought that the noise and the scene she saw must be part of her dream.

But Rachel wasn't sleeping; she dropped the phone and sank in slow motion to the floor. A single wordless sound caught in her throat.

Oh God, oh God, oh God . . .

Reality crept in to her heroin-laced brain. She saw Jessica, lifeless, cradled in a blanket. A single gunshot had ripped her left cheek off and penetrated her skull. Tiny hands, black with gun powder, rested in a pool of her own blood next to Tiana's gun. The pop, the thud; her dream, her child.

Baby . . .

"Baby?"

The Glass Wall

Leslie Dillon knotted her coat at the waist as she hurried from her car and into the YWCA to get out of the Minnesota deep freeze. Once in the door, she snatched a deep breath of warm air and blew it out with a heavy sigh. Glenda, the pleasant desk person who greeted her three times a week, spoke her name and asked if she would like coffee. Leslie nodded that she would and smiled at the thought of what Glenda must think of her. In the six weeks that she had been coming to the Y, she had never even changed clothes at the gym, let alone exercised there.

Her intentions to run the treadmill or walk the track had fallen by the wayside on that very first day when she discovered the racquetball court. She had been wandering through the facility and had heard the sounds of grunting women with racquets hitting a blue ball against the front wall of an enclosed court. One of the side walls of the well-lit box was made of thick glass, and there were bleachers nearby shrouded in darkness. Leslie slowed first to listen then watch the women strategically position the ball in various places around the court to catch their opponent off guard.

Whether it was the certainty with which the women played or the darkness beyond the glass wall at the top of the bleachers, Leslie found the scene curious and comforting. She stood indecisively between the court and the bleachers. She could move forward past the players or climb up onto the wooden benches. She chose the top of the stands. The court noises resonated like echoing thunder and rumbled in her chest. As she observed the explosive sounds from her position behind the glass wall, Leslie felt a moment of peace. It was a feeling she had not been able to embrace since before the day—*that* day—when her life had instantly become a mere line drawing of her once three-dimensional existence.

From her perch, she had heard the players discuss their next game date and knew that she would again come to sit behind the glass wall and watch their match unfold. She decided to come back to this odd place of peace and somehow resurrect her now-devastated life. She was determined to find a space here that matched her pain; she would solve the puzzle she had become. She had existed once. And she had been fearless. Don't forget fearless, she thought.

When she sat in the inky black isolation, she could remember without tearing at her clothing for breath or screaming without pause for life. In this safe and enveloping cocoon of glass and wood, she could place her trembling fingers around the artery of memory that plagued her and from there, decide what to keep, what to throw away. Watching the strength of these opponents reminded Leslie that there was life, perhaps even life worth living, after being raped.

Until the very moment that she settled herself onto the top bench for the first time, she had not allowed herself to think about living or about dying. She had not given one iota of herself over to the terror and disgust that came with the memory of the knife against her temple or the man's penis ripping its passage between her legs. To survive, Leslie had successfully separated her stable and contented lesbian life from the single horrific act that threatened her existence. She now kept her mind and body occupied with an eclectic array of busy-ness. She did everything—anything—but speak.

She found odd outlets of behavior in which to pour her terrifying energy. She cleared her throat incessantly and developed a tic that caused her to duck her head; her once-ambling walk took on a darting, zigzagged gait, as she looked first over one shoulder then the other. At night, she paced and read and stared toward the now-empty side of the bed where her lover had once slept. She showered three times daily and scrubbed at the red and raw patches of broken skin on the inside of her thighs until she bled. She had not even glanced in a mirror since hours before the rape.

She somehow knew that as long as she refused to speak of the atrocity, then she would not crack wide open—that it had not happened—and she could cling to an unnamed source of resilience. Not uttering the words meant that she, not her rapist, would choose her fate. And Leslie could face the damages of her silent, self-imposed choice. It was the uncontrollable noise that she could not endure; the sounds of human betrayal that rang in her memory, waiting to escape from her lips and steal her breath.

On racquetball days, she sat and concentrated on each of the players' strategy. She knew that they were unaware of her existence at the top of the bleachers and that knowledge bolstered and shielded her somehow. It gave her room to reflect on the memories of her whole- ness. The tiniest of incidents might send her flying back toward a safer and more solid patch of her past life. For instance, it occurred to her on one of those early mornings that there was something fragile and sweet about the way one of the players said the word "point." It reminded Leslie of the first girl she had ever kissed. As the past broke the surface, she fluttered her eyes shut, lashes to lids, and wandered into the memory of the toothy, moist-mouthed teenager who had waited with lips slightly parted. She remembered the kiss, watching it over and over again, as she roamed the black screen behind her eyelids for every trace of that first tryst. She bargained for another moment before she transported herself back into the gym. Then, eyes pried open, she again kept her unspoken story weighted onto her shoulders as it reignited the aching in her bones and chest.

She remembered incidentals such as the kiss and avoided the obvious memory of the assault. It was in this tender and tenuous tangle that she learned to lie to her own soul for the sake of what little sanity she had left. This precarious method of deception was meant to evade the monsters of her memory. In truth, Leslie did not know what was real anymore. She only knew that she must get into the gymnasium and climb the steps to her lofty post, to the place where she ordered her silence to protect and serve her until she could find or create a voice she recognized. She also thought about things while she folded her- self onto the top bleacher. She thought about the handwritten note she mailed to her employer and about the friends who had finally stopped trying to reach her. She noticed how little she cared about those once important things that were now only thoughts in her head.

Then, there were times when she thought about her lover . . . ex-lover, Catherine.

Catherine had gone to Seattle because Leslie's voice, unfamiliar and fractured, swore upon all that was holy that she did not love her any more. She had dialed the number and after several rings, Catherine answered. Two hours after a man's penis penetrated her for the first time in her life, a strained and disoriented Leslie spoke into the phone and told her partner that she would not be home.

"What are you talking about, Lee?"

There was a time when Leslie loved to hear her name shortened by her lover. It was an intimacy unshared by any other, and it caused a loving bond to form each time she said it. However, this time,

Catherine's voice reminded her that the world's collective heart was still beating and Leslie would not take part in any such absurdity.

"Catherine, you have to get out of the . . . out of my . . . house. Now. I mean it. It's over. We're over. I hate it, I can't stand the thought of . . ." With a voice beyond her own recognition, Leslie panted and puked the most tyrannical rage toward the woman she loved until Catherine dropped her defense and cracked into slivers of pain.

Although the tremors in her own voice betrayed her words, Catherine spoke carefully and deliberately.

"I know that you love me, Leslie, and I know you don't want to hurt me. Please tell me what's wrong."

There was a pause as the wind howled through the telephone booth. Leslie leaned on the short counter next to the phone book and wondered if she might faint. She squeezed her eyes shut until the tiny space righted itself and then spoke the last words she ever intended to utter.

"There is someone else, Cat. From now on, there always will be."

As Catherine heaved the stale air from her stomach into the phone receiver, Leslie felt the desecration of semen and blood run down the calves of her legs. She gently caressed the mouth of the phone with her fingertips before placing it into its cradle. The whistling gale that hammered into the booth whipped Leslie's hair across her face as she stared at the disconnected receiver now back in its proper place.

For Leslie, the end of life was nothing more than a mad and howling wind.

CR∽ᏸ℘

Whack! The racquetball smacked against the side wall and one of the women, Kelly, dove toward it, tumbling onto the court. She screamed, "Good God, you're amazing! How can you be that strong?"

The other player, Rachel, smiled and replied, "Keeping company with the right women, I guess."

The two exchanged a glance that caused Leslie to question whether or not they were lovers. No, she thought, they're friends who have lovers at home.

Rachel was tall and lean with a muscular frame and easy gait. Her opponent, Kelly, was about the same height but heavier and wider. With her long black ponytail flying, Kelly had more talent for the game than her physical body portrayed. She was quick and relentless with her corner shots. Rachel, on the other hand, had a softer touch with the

racquet; more finesse and less strength. Together, they had developed
a complex game of strategy that benefited both of them each time
they played. At times, they were oddly interchangeable—probably
from years of playing the sport together—and seemed to enjoy one
another's company. Leslie thought about the sounds of their voices
and the genuine comfort she felt while listening to the banter. Their
lives and relationships were still in motion, much like the dark blue
ball that recklessly spun between them.

Her life, on the other hand, was a broken record playing her
insanity over and over again. After six weeks of silent terror,
Leslie could no longer imagine hearing the sound of her own voice.
She thought of answering the phone every time it rang but knew if
she did, the masquerade would be over and the truth would split her
in two. She would not allow herself the luxury of screaming out
the horrific moments that now defined the edge to which she stood so
close.

The panic attacked her daily and sent her wild heart beating into
her wordless throat. When it seized her, Leslie clung to the sole thread
of her salvation, the women on the court. She relied on them to play
the game, hit the ball, win the point, and balance the pain. They
became her eyes and ears, hands and skin. She existed only to watch
them and, in turn, they kept her alive with their strength and stamina.
Her connection to the court warriors was ethereal and it sustained her
on those days when she didn't see them. She could imagine them,
muscles taut and ready, waiting to pounce on the next person who
might hurt her. Always expecting the unthinkable, they shielded her
while she floundered and fled from her senses. They walked beside
and behind her, they cleared the path in front of her, and they lay next
to her while she made unsuccessful attempts to sleep.

When she thought of the racquetball women, Leslie believed that
she might survive. Then she would remember the horrific days just
after the assault before she had discovered her protectors. One of those
days etched in her memory was the day Catherine had left. After their
phone booth conversation, Leslie sat in her car a few blocks from their
home and waited to watch her lover leave. Eyes wide and gripping the
wheel, she clenched her teeth until she thought they would break as
she saw the beautiful woman she cherished put her suitcases into the
trunk, twenty-six hours after the call.

Almost gone. Almost gone. Alllmmmossstt . . . gonnnnne. Leslie
had mentally chanted the words in a sing-song pattern until the sound
of her song drowned out the fury of the man-noises in her head.

Shut up, bitch, and lay . . . almost go . . . *do what I tell* . . . ne, almost gone . . . *you fuckin' whore* . . . almost gone, almost . . . *so tight piece of pusssssssssy* . . . almost gone, almost, gone, almost gone . . . *I'm gonna cum* . . . almost, almost, almost, gone, gone, gone.

She saw her lover drive away from the curb, and then Leslie lay across the front seat of her car in a fetal position. She studied her legs, scratched and bruised, scabs forming on each knee, and reasoned if she could die at that moment, she wouldn't have to enter the empty house. With nothing but the sound of the droning car in her ears and the face of her rapist in her head, the shame in Leslie's chest planted itself into the deepest fiber of lung and refused to go. It was these cruel shards of reality that caused her to careen into the unfamiliar abyss. She was insane, and there was no one to tell. She would rather die than tell.

Get up, she thought, get up and go home, where you will be safe.

Leslie, like most people drowning in madness, did have lucid moments over those first few homebound days. She wrote to her boss and said she had accepted another position, apologizing for her abrupt departure. She put a note on her door saying she had gone to visit friends out of town. But, inevitably, after finishing an apparently ordinary task, she again descended into hell. There was no safety in her home or in her thoughts; no reprieve from the endless, mind-snapping, terror-stricken words and feelings that plagued her.

She refused to turn on a light or go near the locked windows or doors. At night, the most unimaginable noises came and confused her.

Were the noises outside? Was *he* outside? *Is he in the house?*

She mostly sat straight up in bed, phone in her lap, and wondered how she would speak if she had to call 911. What would she say? Could she scream? Would that alone bring them to find her clutching at her own throat to stop the shrieking? Could? Would? With these open-ended questions adding to her madness and no voice to stop the insanity, Leslie knew she was going to die. Her rapist's voice spoke that truth to her again and again.

Then, on the morning of the fifth day, she dozed. It was only thirty minutes or so, but when she woke, startled, she knew she had to get out of the house. She showered and scrubbed, pretending to be late for work, and grabbed her keys. She had discovered that if she hurried, life felt more manageable somehow. As Leslie ran out the door and into the almost sunlit morning, she thought about what might seem conventional to do, like other people; other women who had not been awake for over a hundred hours.

Exercise? Yes, they exercise, she reasoned.

She looked at her still-bruised and swollen legs and a memory choked its way up toward her consciousness.

No, she thought, I will not run outdoors. Not ever again.

She rummaged through the glove compartment and found the YWCA card she had not used since it opened over a year ago.

The Y was a mile or so away but, as she double-checked the locks on her car doors, it never occurred to her to take a change of clothes. She had a mission. She was going to exercise.

Now, several weeks later, Leslie had made a secret nest for herself in the rafters of the racquetball courts, and no one knew how or where to find her. She justified her actions by telling herself that she was going to outlive the terror and shame. Her silence kept her hidden in grief and insanity. Incredibly, Leslie began to think that her life was going well.

Whatever Leslie believed about her existence, she was not any match for what fate and nature were about to bring. It was a clear morning when she entered the gym, took her coffee from Glenda, and headed for the court.

Play was already in progress as she rounded the corner of the hall, and the players were focused entirely on the spinning ball. A slight and undefined recognition tickled the back of Leslie's brain and tugged at her senses, causing her to stop in front of the glass wall. She stared at the court as she strained to identify the sights and sounds of what she saw. Something was different and it scared her. What was it?

Never mind it, she thought, just get up the stairs where it is safe.

Leslie turned to climb the bleachers and heard her player, Kelly, speak words that she suddenly realized she had taken in at least a hundred times in the last several weeks.

"Good God, you're amazing! How can you be that strong?"

The other player, Rachel, smiled and replied, "Keeping company with the right women, I guess."

Leslie turned back toward the court and watched Kelly dive again toward the ball.

"Good God, you're amazing! How can you be that strong?"

Leslie held her breath.

Rachel again smiled and said, "Keeping company with the right women, I guess."

Stumbling toward the glass wall, Leslie searched the women on the court for some change from the last time she had seen them and today. Again, Kelly dove.

"Good God, you're amazing! How can you be that strong?"

Rachel smiled. "Keeping company with the right women, I guess."

A cold chill of awareness shot down her spine and her limbs shook.

Rachel and Kelly always wore the same clothing.

"Good God, you're amazing! How can you be that strong?"

Leslie pressed into the wall to keep from falling and began to beat on the glass with her fists to gain the attention of her protectors.

"Keeping company with the right women, I guess."

The visions on the court slipped from her eyes and her mind flooded with memories of her attacker. Tendrils of terror wrapped around her legs and arms. She flailed herself harder and faster against the glass wall.

The women, now faceless, turned toward Leslie and stood motionless while she stared into them, pounding her flesh and pulling her hair. A scream, raw and desperate, soaked into the corners of the court and over the bleachers as Leslie careened into the glass and broke her nose. Again and again, she banged her head and shoulders toward the players, attempting to reach her only sanctuary of sanity. She clamped her eyelids shut and covered her ears to stop the brutal assault of sound that entered into her. Urine ran down her legs, and an insidious throbbing persisted between them; still, the scream continued.

Finally, Leslie slid down the wall and onto her knees, blood trailing her to the floor, as she realized the scream was from her own throat. She stopped her wounded screams, and, for the first time since she could remember, she began to cry.

Eyes shut, bloody and bruised, alone and broken, Leslie Dillon had found her voice.

CR∽⚜∾⚜∾8O

She rocked and wept with swollen fists balled into her eyes. Her guardians—the women on this court—had been her sanity, and the truth was that they didn't really exist. After several shaky breaths, Leslie found the strength she needed to face that truth. She dropped her fists from her face and opened her eyes. Staring straight into reality, Leslie clearly saw that the racquetball court was empty and dark.

She blinked and stared again to be certain. Even as her body shook in confusion, her mind began to clear a path of acceptance. Breathe deep, she thought, and let it come. She stood, still shaking, while the blood from her nose ran down her shirt and chest. She gazed into the quiet court and cried softly until she felt a hand on her shoulder. Startled, Leslie turned toward the touch and her eyes fell onto the face of the woman she had watched leave their home just weeks earlier.

Leslie wrestled with her demon memories as she looked for signs of forgiveness on Catherine's face.

God forgive me, I can't tell her, she thought, I can't even speak.

Then she remembered the words of her warriors. "Good God, you're amazing! How can you be that strong?"

She realized that they had been speaking those words of encouragement to her. The women wanted Leslie to know that she was full of an amazing strength. They wanted her to recognize their echoing voices as a part of her and, having heard them, know that she would live again. Relief washed over her as tears streamed down her face while she focused on her lover's eyes. Her body continued to shake and she wondered how Catherine had found her and what she must think. Say something, she coaxed herself, say anything to let her know that you're here now, that you love her, that you're sorry. Leslie willed her mouth to form the words but the only sounds that came were sobs of suffering being released.

Finally, Catherine quietly spoke.

"May I touch your face, Lee?"

These words brought another wave of tears from Leslie as she slowly nodded and then waited for Catherine's hands to soothe her. As Catherine reached for Leslie, she softly cried at the sight of this woman she loved so deeply. As she held her face and stroked her hair, she again spoke.

"Can you tell me?"

Leslie visibly relaxed as Catherine caressed her skin and she again looked for her voice. The echoes of the women on the court played in her head as she met her partner's gaze.

"Catherine, I was raped."

Leslie watched the startled look on Catherine's face come and go as she struggled to tell the story for the first time as it happened. She did not take her eyes from her even when the intensity of Catherine's tears matched her own. After she had spoken the last words of the memory, both women stood motionless, drenched in the sad and simple truth.

Finally, Catherine opened her mouth to speak and Leslie heard the most amazing and comforting words that perhaps she had ever heard in her life.

"Good God, you're amazing! How can you be that strong?"

Leslie stared at her beautiful girlfriend and knew that she would spend a lifetime trying to explain just how much those words meant to her. Holding Catherine's hands tighter than she ever had, she replied, "Keeping company with the right women, I guess."

The Last Row of Wheat

The spit of Oklahoma land just north of the Texas border near Lake Texoma is a family farm where I worked off most of my teenage angst. The land is flat and dismal but the fences are well kept and, from a crop duster, the 400-acre parcel looks like a large, oddly shaped bell ringing toward the east. Two barns hold most of the feed for the winter as well as a few milking stalls and there are sweet-smelling haylofts in both. The south barn houses my uncle's tractor and just outside is a combine for baling. The house is a white monstrosity with a picket fence, six bedrooms, and the biggest kitchen I have ever seen; its windows and porch, front and back, are large and give the house a feeling of openness and light.

If I stand between the two barns, just east of the house, I can see the wheat stalks that are planted into the prairie land. I began coming to this farm when I was six and now, twelve years later, my routine is inked into my life and standing between the barns every workday is one of my oldest habits. By 6:30 a.m., after I have tended to the yard animals, my uncle has gassed his machines and given instructions to the four field hands that he has hired for the summer. Then we converge on the house where there are plates of meat, eggs, pancakes, toast, homemade jams and jellies that cover the table. Talk is mostly about the day ahead unless there has been some event of interest like last year when Watson's farm burned nearly to the ground after he got drunk and left a lamp cooking in his barn. Most folks believed it was because his wife was keeping company with the used car lot manager in town but my uncle said that what she did was nobody's business. With breakfast over, all hands went out the door and I followed as far as the spot between the two barns where I stood and watched them enter the wheat fields. I would be expected out in the field around 10 a.m. to drive tractor or bundle bales while my uncle changed jobs to relieve his sciatica. Until then, my time was my own and I often spent it reading behind the north barn, at least, until this particular day.

Now, I am no longer a young woman but the events of that summer, especially on that morning, live with me as if they happened just last week. I can close my eyes and feel of the warm morning sun with the smell of the fields to flood my senses. Those luscious and distinct sensations of the farm are not, however, my most vivid memory—she is.

It was close to hot by the time the hands walked into the neat field rows that morning. As I watched them disappear through the head-high grasses, I knew that the drone of the combine would start soon. From the last row of wheat, an unfamiliar silhouette walked toward instead of away from me and, since it was such an unusual occurrence, I squinted hard to see the stranger. I did not know it then but the nineteen-year-old woman moving toward me so confidently was more than a vision; she was a curious map of sorts that would lead me into my adult life.

With raven hair flowing carelessly down her back, the woman sauntered across the yard and headed directly toward me. Her sleeveless shirt was tied at the waist and blue-jean shorts revealed beautifully tanned arms and legs, but it was not her physical appearance I found so mesmerizing. It was the way she moved into the earth as if she owned it somehow or was an integral part of its creation. I stood transfixed, anticipating the moment she would reach me and the sound of her voice when she spoke.

When close enough to communicate, her soft, gray-blue eyes dug into mine and searched for recognition. She smiled when she found it but, at that time, I could not say what it was that she saw in me. Only steps away, she slowed to a stop and casually dropped her hands into her back pockets causing her breasts to stretch the buttons of the thin cotton shirt.

"*Hi.*"

When I didn't speak but simply stared, she laughed ever so slightly and made a second attempt.

"*Hi? I'm Veronika but most everyone calls me Nika. I am Dalton's daughter from across your east side over there. Our pasture is up against you.*"

"Up against . . . ? Oh! Sorry, I . . . uh, my name is . . . I'm . . . Morgan, Hank Emerson's niece from Illinois, Morgan Hunter. You can call me either. I answer to both."

"*Well . . . Hunter,*" she smiled, "*how long have you been here?*"

"I, uh . . . what? Oh, I come here every summer from Boston to help out. My uncle is my mother's brother."

Nika Dalton seemed amused at my words or perhaps it was my mouth that she found humorous. Either way, she was concentrating on watching me speak and I felt strangely exposed. I glanced toward my shoes to be certain I was still wearing clothes while the slightest hint of anticipation gathered at the base of my throat and traveled down in to my stomach. I wanted her to speak again, to look at me longer, or anything to keep her within breathing distance. I was in unknown territory but it felt strangely familiar. I took a deep breath and, leveling my gaze at her, began to speak again.

"Did you just move here or have we just missed each other all of these years?"

Nika returned my steady gaze for a long moment before she spoke. "*Oh, I would've found you years ago, had I been here. You can count on that.*"

A spark of electricity danced in the pause between us.

"*As it is, my father bought the place last year and moved the family from Wisconsin. I am home from college for the summer and came over to meet you.*"

"Me? How do you know me?"

"*I don't. But I saw you yesterday afternoon in the east field on the tractor. You look,*" she paused to search my face, hoping to find the right word, "*really . . . good . . . on a tractor.*"

I watched her carefully to see whether or not she was going to laugh but her eyes only pulled me into her and held me close. At that moment, I had been unexpectedly transported further away than I had ever gone from everything I had ever known and I realized that I was anxious to go. Standing just a foot away, I was surprised to suddenly imagine how her body might fit into my mine and I breathed her in until the heat of my skin began to overtake the warmth of the day. How long we stood there was impossible to determine and I remember nothing of what was said until she casually put her hand on my hat and, as she slid it back, said, "*I know you, Hunter. Really I do. And you are going to know me; you understand that, yes?*"

"I don't know if I do . . . understand you, I mean."

"*Have . . . you . . . ever . . . ?*" she whispered.

"Nika, I . . . no, I . . . ." I interrupted.

"*You don't even know what I was going to say, do you?*"

I put on my best smile and slowly shook my head.

"Well, I want to say something and I want you to listen, ok? Carefully. Watch my lips."

I fixed my gaze onto her mouth and held my breath.

"Are you watching?" she asked quietly.

I nodded, captivated by the plumpness of her bottom lip and how her wet tongue teased at the back of her teeth when she whispered again.

"Come with me," she murmured.

My hands instinctively reached for her and stopped just short of the tight shirt. We both looked down toward my trembling fingers, realizing that a step closer would send us far away from the space between those two barns. Nika trembled slightly, then abruptly recovered and slid her hand off of my hat, onto my shoulder, and down my side until it fell naturally back into her own jurisdiction.

"What do you mean, 'come with you'?" I cautiously asked.

Again, her mouth trembled slightly and, just before speaking, she thoughtfully outlined the curve of her top lip with her right forefinger.

"Tomorrow afternoon. Come with me out to our back pond. No one ever goes out there and it is a great place to . . . swim. You do swim, don't you?"

"I . . . I . . . ssw . . . sswww . . . swim," I stammered.

"Great," I inwardly scolded, "I'm an idiot."

I was grateful that she did not comment on my stuttering tongue, simply choosing to smile instead. Nika was the wiser of us during this ancient mating ritual and I, her novice, became her cloak and dagger—her sheltering cover and the razor sharp edge of her desire. She tossed and turned me, carving her sensuality into my muscles and bones until I was reduced to a sexual mass of stuttering being.

We stood aching, embraced by the sun, and she eyed me steadily, spoke so quietly, until I could hardly stand the empty space between us. Then she backed away slowly, finally turned, and entered the last row of wheat. As I watched her float into the farmland, I wondered for an instant if the whirlwind that had just happened was real and whether I would actually see her again.

My attraction for her was immediate and quite natural, therefore, completely without judgment. Like most of life when it twists and changes so abruptly, I had no time to figure the rules or consequences. I began my journey with Nika the same way an avid reader might sit down with a fresh, new novel; I was open to any and all of the possibilities that lay just beneath her cover.

Now, this might be the natural place to discuss my fear and trepidation about loving a woman but truthfully, I had little thought about anyone who was not her. I knew that no one could understand how she fitted into me and I was not wired to explain it to them. I quickly decided to leave shame and guilt for my mother's other children who had lives that could accommodate such nonsense. While my life has taken on plenty of changes over these thirty years, I am still not inclined to seek forgiveness for the most solid side of me. Besides, loving a woman has been the deepest, most satisfying, part of my living. The right woman will set a fire under my skin until it burns slow with haunting memories of how she moves to take me into her. The sound of her breathlessness will keep me awake and yearning for hours. These are the lessons that Nika Dalton bundled up and brought to me and I am—have always been—eternally grateful to her for it.

ᏯᎥᎿᏍᏓ

When my mother asked me to go out into the west field to bring my father in for supper, I was glad for the distraction. I had been stuck for hours in the kitchen on the south side of the house soaking cucumbers for canning. While I didn't mind the work, I smelled of vinegar and my back ached. I was ready to walk those hundred acres and stretch my legs a bit. I grabbed a straw hat and a cold drink, stepped onto the back porch, and breathed deeply. The brutal heat of the day was fading as the sun slipped itself toward the earth's pocket and the smell of dusty wheat emptied into the air.

This farm would not have been my first choice but my middle-aged parents had taken to it almost instantly. "Nika, your parents, Ruby and Silas, are tired of the city," they exclaimed as if they were gossiping about another couple, "and they want you to know that they are buying the farm." My father thought that this tasteless play on words was hilarious but I refrained from encouraging his juvenile humor. If they wanted to reenact "Green Acres," I had little to say about it, that is, until I went to the farm to spend the summer after my sophomore year in college. I had escaped to Europe during my freshman summer but could find no excuse not to join them the following year in, of all God forsaken places, Oklahoma. It was hardly what I expected although, looking back, I am not sure what it was I had anticipated.

The most overwhelming part of the farm was the work it took to keep it moving. There was always something that had to be done and mostly we were on the verge of being late in doing it. Daily harvesting,

weekly canning, monthly planting, not to mention washing, painting, feeding, baling, mending, shucking, cleaning, storing; it was
endless. After a while, I suppose I got used to it. I was not opposed
to hard work; it was the eternal prospect of it that plagued me. There
was that during the day, but it did little to occupy my nineteen-year-
old lesbian body during the night.

Oh, the nights! Once the sun started to set in the western fields,
the moon took its rightful place in the crystal sky and it was then that
my memory began to throb and toss images of big, muscular girls and
their strong hands everywhere, anywhere on my body. I had ripened
under the touch of lesbians who knew how to hold me, reach for me,
and I longed to feel their solid presence again. Forget love. I was
much more interested in the restless and tender pains of desire that
brushed up against my skin until the early hours of morning, leaving
me raw and somehow alert even as I dreamt. My "day-long work" and
"night-long craving" personas coexisted rather fitfully until the late
afternoon when Ruby Dalton sent me, her only child, to fetch Silas for
supper.

Coming upon the clearing of the west field, I casually glanced
toward the Emerson's east field and saw what I thought might be
a mirage. Several field hands were on the ground, turning the wheat
as the tractor came through and combing the stalks. But it was the
tractor, actually, the young woman—girl, perhaps—on the tractor that
caused me to study the earthy lines of her horizon for any recognition
of who she might be. I moved closer toward the field and stood
behind the last oak tree on our property until I could see the sweat
fall onto her collar from her short-cropped hair; arms and legs—
trees of her own—commanding the will of the tractor; squeezing,
pushing, kneading, stroking the machine with firm and comfortable
grips. Her dark skin rippled in the blaze of sunset and I knew that not
another day would pass before I knew who she was and how I would
know her.

That is how it began for me in the summer of my truest desire. I
did not know it then but, years later, Morgan Hunter would become
the fullness that would replace most of my hollow and empty shadows.
On this day, however, my goal was to meet the girl next door and,
tomorrow, if I finished all I had to do early enough, I could accomplish
that feat.

As I walked through the last row of wheat that morning, I almost
laughed out loud at how nervous I felt. "She may not even be a
lesbian," I warned myself. "No, that would be impossible. I wonder if

she knows yet. How old is she? What am I doing to myself with all of these questions?" I thought. "Good question," I answered.

Trying to decide what to wear on this morning was just as confusing as all of the questions. Shirt? Sleeveless? Sundress? No. Shorts . . . short shorts. Too obvious? Yes. In that case, by all means, I'll wear them.

I tied my shirt up and onto my stomach as I walked along the last few yards of the wheat row and wondered where I might find her. Moments later, my answer was standing between the barns and directly in front of me just about fifty feet away. I moved toward her and questioned whether she knew I was coming somehow and was waiting for me but then realized just how crazy that was. I have since learned, of course, that desire has its own radar, far more sophisticated than we can ever know.

I slipped my hands into my back pockets so that she wouldn't see me trembling and introduced myself. She hesitated and I had the opportunity to see up close what I had only imagined the day before. Her blue black hair was thick and tousled, arms and hands brown and bulked from working in the sun, and powerful legs that stretched the cotton of her khaki shorts. I caught the scent of her morning shower mingled with clean sweat and laughed slightly to cover my shallow breathing. When she did not speak, I again introduced myself and she suddenly spilled over, telling me her name and who her uncle was and how long she had been coming to the farm. I tried to pay attention to her words but her mouth had my attention and I could think of nothing other than tracing her lips with my fingers. I would've said anything to keep her talking, to watch the words tumble out from between her teeth, surrounded by that beautiful, beautiful mouth. She was a lesbian all right and, as I pushed her hat back and flirted with her to come to the pond with me the next day, it suddenly and instinctively occurred to me that I was about to become Morgan Hunter's first experience. That revelation startled me and I felt myself shiver from something that I could not yet identify. As I turned to leave, a part of me stayed there next to her and, for the first time in my own young lesbian life, I felt incomplete.

ଔ෴ଐ

Nika and I were joined by forces, ethereal and earthy—forces that blew a dense sensuousness into our every breath. I had no explanation for it and did not need one. However, there is little doubt that when such intervention occurs, there is no space for the daily ticking of clocks. She was my first and last thought and her physical presence became my only requirement. But I am ahead of myself.

When the next afternoon came, I bolted from the farm and toward the pond like my hair was on fire. Down the last row of wheat and through the east field, I hurdled Dalton's fence and skirted the edge of the property, avoiding the house, the barn, and the people who were possibly in either. I slowed to a trot when I entered the wooded path, careful not to get caught in the brambles and thought, "Another sixty seconds and I will see her again." Just as quickly, a second thought not nearly so pleasant followed. "I forgot my bathing suit. Damn, damn, damn it."

CR∙◈∙ED

I sat, feet and ankles dangling into the pond, and looked at my watch again. I wondered if Hunter would come or if I had scared her half to death. I had hurried through chores, breaking a couple of eggs along the way, and almost spilled half of a five gallon bucket of milk. Smiling at the memory, I looked around for signs of her and inhaled the brilliant display of scenery around me. The hot and wet summer had filled and saturated this plump trace of land nestled in the forest. Thickets were heavy with berries and the trees' canopy hung bowed and bent with thick, luscious leaves. The carpet of the clearing was a padded mixture of pungent moss and slick, sweet grasses pressed into the swollen and muddied earth. The pond water was still and warm, patiently waiting for Hunter and me to slowly sink into her saturated belly.

"I forgot my suit."

The brush parted at the trail and I must've looked startled because Hunter fought off a smile and continued walking toward me.

"Should I go back? It would only take about half an hour or so. I'll hurry."

She turned to go and I heard the urgency in my own voice. "No, please, wait." *I slowed and took a breath.* "You won't need a suit. It is just the two of us out here. Even the cows don't come out this far from home."

CR∙◈∙ED

To explain how a woman might touch another woman may be treading on sacred ground for some but something must be said in order to understand the impact, the whole affect, of the two together. It is not discussed in ways that would describe a physical sound or movement; it is more about the position of the heart when her fullness comes into you that will capture you and take you in. This reckless and inevitable dance is love, truly, and it is what we made, indeed.

When Nika rushed to stop me from leaving the pond, I felt her in my very core, her hands and mouth soothing me long before she ever touched me. It was then that I knew I would love her and, at that moment, I understood more about physical loving than I ever thought I would. The mystery was soon to be over and I had made a place in my heart for the knowledge of it.

She stepped into me as she spoke something about cows and I felt her breath on my cheek. I watched her lips move as her arms nestled around my neck and landed comfortably into position on my shoulders. She smelled of wheat and dust; her hair was feather-soft and fell onto the curve of my breasts. I hooked my fingers into her back belt loops and rested my hands softly on the lower part of her bare back. My heart moved from one place to the next; first, to the soft and low sound of her, then to the firm and willing feel of her.

"*Wait,*" she whispered. "*I want you to remember this, always.*"

Nika turned her head so slightly and allowed her eyes to return my gaze. "I promise. I will," I told her, and a slow burn began moving in my belly and through my legs and arms as I lowered my head to bring her mouth onto mine for the first time.

ଓ๛ଆ

I instinctively moved toward Hunter as she came through the clearing and threw my arms around her neck. My desperation to have this woman's hands on me felt almost dangerous and I clung to her, working to catch my breath, while she let her fingers dangle gently on the skin of my back. I stepped away enough to see the haunted hunger in her eyes and watched her handsome face move toward my mouth. I wanted her to remember that kiss always and told her so; she promised that she would.

Slipping out of my own clothes and watching her undress her muscular, brown body was a powerful exercise in patience for both of us. Although it was painful to stay at such a slow and steady pace, I was determined to keep her moving with me, time and again, until she understood how to please me, herself, and us. Each kiss, every glance—the sweat and tears—her hands, her body inside of me, solid, and strong; I was cocooned in her arms and legs for the hours to pass without noticing, without needing any more than we had already found.

೦ಹ~ॐ~ಕ್ಷಿ

There was no steadiness to my breath when I reached into her; my own unbridled body aching, arching with obsession, moment by moment, again and still again. But Nika held me infinitely still until I understood where and how to bring her, myself, and us to an unquestionable fulfillment that I came to understand and appreciate that afternoon. She eased her sweet, wet tongue between my teeth and stroked the inside of my mouth, urging me to come closer, wait longer, thrust harder. I followed her lead toward the future and I vowed to stay as long as she, who was teasing and taking me toward my own destiny, would allow it.

೦ಹ~ॐ~ಕ್ಷಿ

Hunter and I spent night after night, day after day, embraced in perfection until I realized I loved her; loved her deeply. It was then that I wondered, "How in the world can I stay?"

೦ಹ~ॐ~ಕ್ಷಿ

Nika and I spent day after day, night after night, surrounded by love, so deeply abiding that it caused her to leave. It was then that I wondered, "How in the world can you go?"

೦ಹ~ॐ~ಕ್ಷಿ

Dreams have no shape or fashion; no time to become outdated or well worn. We mostly just tuck them into the tattered seams of our lives to repair the rips that living tears in to us. My summer with Hunter was a glorious dream; one that later soothed the cracks of my heart and filled my lonely nights as I compared my last real date to my only true love. After that awakening with her, I became terrified of the true feelings that I felt and convinced myself that we were entirely wrong for each other. I crushed her with words like "too young" and "too different" and "puppy love." To convince myself that I had done the right thing, I even settled for less than I deserved, at least, for a while. When my father died, I came back to this Oklahoma farm and ran it with my mother until she too was gone. I always thought I would sell the place but could never bring myself to do it. At least a few times a month I would walk down the last row of wheat and stare between the two barns until I could conjure up the image of a young Hunter, waiting for me in the hot morning sun. These are the notions that occupied my mind as I marked the time passing; the Emersons had died long ago and Hunter, last I heard, was in Seattle with a lover or partner, I assumed. A Christmas card or a note from a vacation was all I had to remind me of the only person I had ever loved so incredibly, the person that I had left so completely.

ᏟᏍᏙ

When Nika told me that we were not going to be together, my heart shattered, leaving thousands of tiny bits for several women to try and patch up over the years. I healed as best I could and my dream of being with her slipped into a quiet pocket of my past. When I was tired or lonely or simply could not stand it any more, I would allow her to surface and possess my memory for a while but never for long. The pain was rugged whenever I allowed my thoughts of that season to linger. During my first few summers of college, I would rush to the farm, hoping to find her but I stopped going when my heart could no longer take the disappointment. Uncle Hank moved to Ohio after his wife died and, when he passed, he left the farm to my mother. She rented out the fields to strangers and closed up the huge, white house. After her death, I became the sole beneficiary of my uncle's farm, although I had not been there in twenty years. I didn't hear from Nika again, save a letter from time to time to update me about the property. I sent a few cards until her parents died and then I assumed she had moved into a city somewhere, probably living with a lover or partner. She never cared much for farming.

ᏟᏍᏙ

At 6 a.m., the summer sun was not yet beating down on the wheat fields. I watched a steady stream of cars moving toward the auction over at the Emersons and guessed that Hunter was finally having the bank dismantle and sell the place. Just about every family farm for miles had been either subsidized or rolled over into a junkyard or used car lot. Soon enough, the vultures would come knocking on my own door and I would have decisions to make. I had hung on to the memories of my parents and my youth long enough, I supposed. It was time to move into a city—maybe Chicago or Boston—and attempt to jump-start my life yet again. By seven, the postman had rung the bell and, when I answered, I don't recall just what he said that caused me to realize Hunter was next door at the auction. In fact, I don't remember combing my hair or changing clothes or flying out the back door to desperately reclaim my heart. I only remember running to her . . .

ᏣᎥᎦᎦᏯ

. . . standing between the barns, I gazed out toward the east field and thought of the hundreds of times I had stood in this very spot. I felt eighteen years old coming back here again and just as raw, looking toward the Dalton place. "Thousands of tiny bits, Nika, and I have yet to put any of me back together," I muttered to myself. The distant sound of the auctioneer faded and the summer breeze caused me to close my eyes and inhale the fullness of my painful memories. As the sun broke over the east field, I turned to move toward the house when, out of the corner of my eye, I caught the silhouette of a woman. She had stepped out of the last row of wheat and, with her raven hair flowing, her sleeveless shirt tied at the waist, Nika came running out of my past and headed straight toward my future.

Sandra Dee's Lips

When you're going to tell a story, for instance, it's better to understand from the beginning that it will become a part of you. If you know that right off the bat, then there is a good chance that you won't fight the particulars when they seep into your memory and bones; you won't be embarrassed by the tenderness it can bring. After a certain age, stories become the solid part of living, taking up space where there was once schedules and heartache. A well-told story has a skin about it that will hold you upright against a lonely night or a raging betrayal. It will bleed for you and, in some stories, bring you just the right amount of love for the day, not to mention an interesting point or two. Story telling, like the one I am about to tell you, is sometimes meant for the faint of heart; the romantic who will sacrifice a few spare moments for a sweetness that can only be found in the words of a stranger.

CR∽ઝ৪৩

My aunt, Lillian Sly, was a woman without the borders of convention. In 1952, when she was twelve years old, she announced to her family and friends—including the minister at the First Presbyterian Church—that she would no longer answer to her given name, Lillian. If those who knew her would not call her "Lil" then she could not be held responsible to answer them. Oh, at first, her mother and father thought little of it, perhaps even found it a bit endearing. However, her older sister, Margaret, had a somewhat sordid theory. She believed, or at least she told everyone, that Lillian had slipped from the doctor's grasp and onto the floor during birth and that was the true malady from which her sister suffered. Although it was not true, Margaret felt relieved when her friends shined sympathy rather than disgust upon her for having such an odd and boisterous sister. Well, the family spent weeks humoring my aunt. Then it turned into an irritating attempt to remember what to call her and ended with an exasperating outburst on an otherwise quiet Sunday afternoon.

"Lillian," my grandmother bellowed, "I am your mother and I will not call you by any name other than your full name, which is a beautiful name; one that I picked out, although your father wanted to name you Ruth. Calling you Lil makes me think you should be wearing a feather boa and belting out bar songs in a saloon and I will not let that thought keep me awake every night for the rest of my life. There is no Lil, my child, only 'Lillian,' and you are her."

Well, my aunt promptly ignored my grandmother and, consequently, spent the next six nights during dinner in her room. My grandfather, the voice of reason, gently spoke to his wife at the end of a very long and disturbing week of evening meals.

"Mary, honey, we cannot continue to keep the child from dinner, can we? Don't you think we need to be concerned about starvation at some point? She looks a little skinnier to me and . . ."

So it was, that Lil came to dinner the next night. And for every day and night thereafter, she would be known, and called, Lil Sly.

Aunt Lil was a square girl who would grow up to be a big, strong, and agile woman. She wore what she wanted, despite the cajoling of her mother and embarrassment of her sister, and she drank heavily at any early age. In high school, her friends were college women and people with jobs in odd places. Her best friend, incidentally mistaken as her boyfriend for years, was Simon, a lanky mortician with a persistent rash on the bridge of his nose from thick black glasses. They would talk for hours about mathematics or Europe while playing chess at the dining room table.

Lil could make me hysterical when I was a girl by imitating my mother; nose in the air with a look that always suggested there was dogshit somewhere within stepping distance of her shoe. She was a loyal friend and companion, a smart and worthy opponent, and a woman steeped in esteem, although God only knows why. It is like that sometimes. Out of an ordinary seed, some act of mystification will collide with a natural kind of fate to form something precious yet, unbreakable. She had no looks to speak of and could not have cared less what others thought of her. She never raised her voice that I can remember and was more honest than any other living soul. That is why it was no surprise when the nineteen-year-old Lil decided to tell her family what it was that she had discovered about herself in 1959.

It was on a Friday in May and, just like every other day, Lil had walked home from her factory job at the Staley plant. Her heart, however, was weary on this particular afternoon from trying to get out of her chest and onto her sleeve. Like sleeping on the unused side of a well-worn bed, she couldn't quite get comfortable in the covers of her skin and finally she knew why. For years, she had known that she was not like other women and it had taken her the better part of that time to figure it out. Despite her mother's pleadings, she had never had a boyfriend and had never wanted one. That part was simple enough and she rarely thought about her future and whether or not she would be lonely. Still, Lil yearned for a life that was not yet defined and she had no words for it, at least until that Friday.

Earlier on that day, Lil sat in the break room drinking the remnants of a cup of coffee she had nursed for most of the morning. The hangover and late night she had was making it hard for her to give a damn one way or another about much of anything. Co-workers, Toni and Lana, walked in the door, followed by a few of the other women coming in for morning break as well. Whether it was fate or God or stars colliding is still a mystery but, in the shortest blink of an eye, Lil glanced up in time to see her future in the shape of one Patsy McGuire. Now, that may sound like a dime store novel but most of life, when told properly, has a lot of dime store qualities to it so bear with me.

Patsy was a gum-chewing, lipstick-laced beauty with an easy gait that caused most people to stop and take notice. She wore bright scarves and tight sweaters with men's pants and red fingernail polish. Rumor had it that she was a war-bride-turned-widow but the truth of the matter was that Patsy had never been married and, believe me, it wasn't in her plans. Lil felt her stomach stir and, for a moment, considered that it might've been last night's highballs. But, as she watched Patsy saunter across the room and throw a knowing glance right back at her, she knew it wasn't the booze at all. Sometimes, when some thing so small occurs, you might wonder if your life would've come out the same if that moment—that event—had not happened. Thankfully, you never know the answers to such questions.

The full feeling of a heart finally set into motion is an enlightening experience. Lil stared at Patsy and every other woman in the room until she came to understand what she had somehow always known. Life had finally righted itself for my aunt and now she had to go about making that life, not with the man of her mother's dreams, but with the woman of her own.

First, however, she had to set the record straight.

When Lil walked in the front door of her childhood home that afternoon, she bellowed for anyone who could hear within a city block. "I need a family meeting after dinner." Then she picked up the phone and called Simon first, and then my mother, Margaret, telling them that she had an announcement and wanted them to come over right after dinner. My mother had married my father nine months before and was now very pregnant with yours truly, due any day, but she agreed to be there at six-thirty. After all, it wasn't every day that Lillian Sly was going to speak to her family and hardly any of them could contain their curiosity. Precisely on the half-hour, everyone gathered with their coffee in the living room and my Aunt Lil delivered this speech.

"It's a simple thing I am about to tell you and you may not understand it. I have come to know something about myself that you should all know as well so you will never have to wonder about me. I do not like men—no offense, Simon—at least, in the ways that most women do but I have discovered that I do like women—in that way. Therefore, I will not be looking for a husband, no small surprise there, but will choose a mate that pleases me from my own sex. There is no one in particular that I am ready to discuss with you at present but, now that I know my true nature, I would expect that I will find my . . . woman . . . in the near future." Lil sat down after speaking what was on her mind and, to this day, my mother still swears that you could hear a hummingbird suckling two houses down.

It is safe to say after that fateful day, the discussions about Lil went on for years but she was not usually in the room at the time. Oh, there was the initial uprising of drama but that's the dime store stuff I spoke of earlier. Mostly, our family was in shock to the point of being stupefied and by the time they were thawed, Lil was in earnest pursuit of Patsy.

Besides, someone actually living an honest life in the Sly household was a novelty and there was much to learn from it. I would venture to guess that Aunt Lil's frank revelation brought a whole new closeness to my nuclear family and, if they would've had the presence of mind to say it, might've thanked her for the fodder. As it was, they just holed up in their houses at the end of the day and whispered aloud what they were truly thinking.

"How do they . . . ?" "Where does she . . . ?" "Can you imagine . . . ?"

But how can anyone truly imagine another person's unbridled joy? And, oh, how joyous they were. Eighteen years, almost to the day, it was that Lil and Patsy were together till 1977 when another act of fate split the pair like ripened halves of a Christmas walnut. It was a day when the particulars of an event would bring my Aunt Lil into a moment of pain that would last her lifetime.

Early on a Saturday when they were supposed to go to breakfast with my mother and father, Patsy woke up before sunrise, complaining of stomach pains. She got up to find Tums and Aunt Lil rolled over to sleep. Two hours later, at six o'clock, Lil found Patsy dead on the bathroom floor from a massive heart attack. She was forty-three years old.

Now, when the heart resigns itself to sorrow, its veins and arteries are filled with a dense and lugubrious grief that changes the very sound of its beating. It is that solemn change in the beating of life that keeps you in mourning long after someone is dead. As you might've guessed, this thick-blooded presence became my Aunt Lil. She walked the streets at night and stood knee-deep in the lake on the west end of town; she sat in the last row of any place she went and did not return phone calls to anyone.

She listened for Patsy and forgot to eat; she drank until she fell asleep sitting at the kitchen table and didn't shower before going to work. She lived without being present until the darkness passed and she finally stopped struggling to see Patsy in everything around her. Life was different but it slowly began to crawl back into its rightful speed. Aunt Lil grew past Patsy's passing but not her memory. She put away her intimacies, trading them for a careful and thorough stance in my eighteen-year-old life; a life that was, well, that's the next part of the story.

CB❦❧BO

There are times when the first thing that happens is the last thing you expect. Then there are other times when the things you thought could never happen, do. Both of these truisms applied to my parents, Douglas and Margaret Atwood, or Dusty and Mitts, as they affectionately referred to each other. In 1958, the first time these two recent college graduates had sex—after marriage, of course—they got pregnant with me. Then in the late 70s, when all of my friends were getting married, I sat down with Dusty and Mitts to inform them that I was a lesbian. My mother commented that she did not know how such a thing could happen again in one family and wondered if it was in our genes or the result of some vitamin that she had taken while pregnant.

My father asked me to go fishing. "Uh, Dad, I said, I'm a lessssbiiiiiaannnn. I like women, not fish."

Thankfully, that was the end of that discussion. After the initial quaking wore off, my family settled into a generic acceptance that there were two lesbians in the family; one at full gallop and the other at the starting gate. My grandmother was sure that having Aunt Lil as one of my role models had somehow affected my ability to be straight but I knew the truth.

I knew back in 1971, when I was twelve years old, that the sound and feel of women would define me and draw me into a place of sensual refuge. The alternative was just too awkward and unnatural to consider. My parents named me Shirley Delores Atwood after the actress Shirley Temple but, like Aunt Lil, I would forever be called Leedee because anything else would, well, just be too awkward and unnatural to consider.

People call me a "beauty," like my mother, and I could sense her uneasiness with the close resemblance ever since she found out that I was girl-crazy. It doesn't fit to her that a beautiful woman, especially one who looks like her, would only have eyes for another woman.

Me, on the other hand, I live for that. I was—and am—an admittedly hopeless romantic. Back then, I was frequently in love again for the last time, and my Aunt Lil was always there with a word of encouragement when I needed it. As far back as my memory stretches, she and Patsy were my mentors, role models and surrogate parents. After I had identified myself as a lesbian and Patsy had died, Lil and I became even closer. I knew that I somehow reminded Lil of Patsy in those first fresh days of grief and, while it might have been a painful awareness for her, she ultimately took comfort in that fact. She looked so intently at me sometimes, like she was catching a glimpse of a familiar ghost, and then she'd fall into a distant stare, shaking it off after a moment or so. Lil never told me what she was thinking at those times. I guess I mostly believed that Patsy was sending her grief-stricken lover a message that there is memory and connection after death, that she is never far away, and that life is worth living because of those very facts. After all, most of the things that we truly know we learned from those who are already gone.

As the grief of Patsy spread through me, I came face-to-face with greatest loss of my young life, my apparent inability to love. Never truly loving is a cruel and square thing. It is hard-edged and razor sharp. Even thinking of it caused me to stumble inward without direction and lose balance. My greatest fear is that I would never know the kind of love that I saw between my aunts and how I ached to have the kind of love that they had experienced. I wanted someone to caress my fingers and bring me spring flowers for no reason at all; someone I would long for until she filled the void that no one else could touch. It seemed, however, that I was just slightly off the mark when it came to finding a mate, especially after Patsy died. The women that I had chosen were strong enough—beautiful in ways that I liked—but when it came right down to it, each one of them had that "something" about her, something that I could not put my finger on, that did not make for a lasting relationship. Then again, maybe it was not the women I had chosen at all. Maybe it was me who placed each relationship under a microscope until I could label it "broken" and shelve it with the rest of the experiments.

It's a sure-fire way to stay away from people if you think about it.

Anyhow, ten years and three broken relationships later, I was twenty-nine years old and sure that I was putting out signals of desperation or some other dysfunction but Lil didn't believe that was the case.

"You're just not ready to see it yet, Leedee." She told me this one rainy afternoon while we were having a late lunch at Swannies' bar beside the plant where Lil worked.

"What 'it,' Lil?" I asked.

"Ah, well now, there's the question, isn't it, Doll?"

"Okay, what's the answer?"

Lil thought for a good long while before she finally spoke.

"Sandra Dee's lips."

Pause.

"What?"

"Sandra Dee's lips."

Well, she had said it again and it made no more sense to me than the first time that she said it.

"I don't real—"

"I had looked at Patsy for months before I truly noticed her, you know? And, when I finally did really see her, the first thing that I noticed was that she had lips like Sandra Dee. Now I can't tell you why that affected me the way it did but I can tell you that, once I saw her lips, all I thought about was kissing her. After that, the rest was easy."

Easy? We obviously didn't know the same women. Just as I was about to speak, Lil raised her hand to stop me.

"Just hang on, Leedee, and see if you can make sense of this. I don't mean that the relationship was easy. Lord knows, in eighteen years, Patsy and I had our ups and downs. But even when things were tough, we managed. That's because we had found something in each other when we first met that was unlike anything else we could've found in anyone else. We hung on to what we'd found, knowing that it could never be replaced. That's what kept us—or any other couple for that matter—together. Take your mom and dad, for instance. Who but Dusty could put up with Mitts, right? When you or I look at your mom, we see a prissy woman with a wide board up her butt but your dad? He sees a young and winsome prom queen with gorgeous eyes. When he remembers what he loves about her, then he remembers to honor her and makes room for her odd and quirky ways. Now, there's a love that lasts, Leedee; an unconditional love that has a long memory about the best of who we are. I got to know the woman behind the Sandra Dee lips and, as a result, fell in love with so much more."

As my aunt spoke, I remembered the number of times I had seen my father softly touch the tiny lines beside my mother's eyes with his forefingers and whisper, "Beautiful," as he passed her in the kitchen or hallway. I felt relieved and embarrassed about realizing the intimacies that I had witnessed for years and wanted to say so but Lil began to hone in on what her point truly was—me.

"I've watched you move in and out of relationships with some pretty fine women, Honey, but never one that you truly saw for who she was. It always looked as if you were working so hard at having the relationship that you forgot that you were supposed to be loving somebody. Before you choose another woman, you may want to know her well enough to see what it is that attracts you. Be ready to accept her as she is, not how you want her to be. That way, when things are tough, you will think the best of her by remembering what you love about her. The relationship will take care of itself."

She was right, of course.

Born a romantic, I also knew that I was less than stellar in the romance department; always getting hung up on the details without truly enjoying the ride. But what if I stopped weighing and measuring every last ounce of each relationship? Wouldn't I have to be vulnerable without knowing that things were going to work out? That's like trusting God or somebody to make sure that the "right" thing is happening to me.

And why in the world would I do that?

Lil read my mind as I was sorting through my possible changes and simply said, "You can't control anything, Leedee. You can only busy yourself thinking that you can. Love somebody, child. Find somebody who makes you forget that you ever wanted any control. That's the woman with Sandra Dee's lips."

Right again.

"What if she dies?" I blurted.

If this question startled Lil, she never let on. She was quiet for a long time before looking me squarely in the eyes. When she spoke, it was quiet and sure.

"We all die, Leedee, that's a fact. Not one of us will take one more breath than God intended. It's what we do while we are here that makes the difference. And it's how we love those we love that matters. The rest is just icing on the cake."

My aunt's words hung with me for the better part of a week as I weighed and examined my carefully measured life. Lil had seemed awfully sure about what I needed but I felt mostly confused and preoccupied which is about how I was one Tuesday afternoon, standing in an uncommonly long line at the corner drug. Holding an armful of necessities, I shuffled through the line as if I were in a concentration camp, staring at the tabloid headlines for signs of my life.

"Excuse me?" I heard a voice surface into my thoughts and furrowed my brow with agitation. Mustering my best intimidation, I slowly turned to level my gaze at the intruder and let her know that I had placed her at end of my "I don't give a shit" list.

You may have guessed by now that that is not what happened at all.

She was the kind of drop-dead gorgeous that only a true lesbian can understand; arms meant to hold someone and enough legs to wrap a body around with a smile that answered every question I had. She was unflappable and my most feeble attempt to give her "the glare" was met with the sweetest dimpled smirk I had ever encountered.

"I . . . uh . . . well, you shou . . . er . . . can I . . . hmmm . . ."

I seemed to have lost my ability to speak and she, standing there grinning, was quite content to let me flounder. That is a trait that I can honestly say she still has to this day, twenty-six years later.

Now, sometimes, the particulars about a story aren't always important; it's more the outcome that's likely to stand out. I could tell you about our first kiss or give you the details of our lengthy and sometimes turbulent courtship. I could spin you a yarn about our many fights or fill you with information about how Mitts and Dusty loved Kit as their own. All of it, however, would pale in comparison to telling you what we created and accomplished in our life together; that together we somehow became lovely and invincible; we defied the laws of emotional gravity and wound up asleep in our own well-worn bed.

From the moment that I knew Kit, I never lost sight of my aunt Lil's words to love and cherish what I loved about her. Years later, watching her in the garden or seeing her doze in her favorite chair, I am struck by her profile, her hands, and the comforting memory of her breath in my hair. My "Sandra Dee lips" are the soft lines around her ever-twinkling eyes and the softness of her cheek. Those particulars of hers have been my mainstay for all these many years, I am a better woman for it, and I owe that bit of insight and wisdom to my aunt Lil.

CR-6·80

Just like any other ending that catches people somewhere between the head and heart, this one is just what you'd expect. Six months ago, Lil called Kit and me to come to dinner at her home. It was the middle of the week and, as anyone from around here knows, there must be something brewing if it's a weekday meal you've been invited to.

After dinner, Lil sat in her rocking chair and, with a distant light in her eyes, she told us that it was almost time for her to become reacquainted with Patsy. The wistful happiness on her face was undeniable as she explained the diagnosis and just how much time she might have left. When she finished speaking, she pulled me into her arms—a gesture that she had become famous for—and whispered into my ear as she held me ever so close.

"I am not worried about you, Leedee, and I don't want you to worry about me either, ok? I am going exactly where I want to go, you understand? And when I do, I promise to take a small piece of your heart with me to share with Patsy until you join us in a hundred years or so."

My tears spilled onto Lil's shirt sleeve as I hugged her tight around the neck.

"How do I do this, Lil? Let you go, I mean? I'll be so scared without you and who will keep me alive and strong?"

Lil shook loose from me enough to hold my face in between her big, warm hands.

"Listen to me, Doll, it's you that's kept me alive and strong for so long. If not for you, I would've ended my life years ago from sheer grief alone. You have never stood in my shadow, girl. You blazed your own trail. I am just the woman who helped you find the path. I promise, you'll be fine."

Well, it was just two Saturdays ago that I sat by Lil's bed, reading one of her favorite stories to her. As I paused to turn a page, I glanced toward the now-small figure propped up between the pillows and instinctively took her hand in mine. Lil stared straight into my eyes and whispered, "I wish you could see her, Leedee. She's still got those lips . . ."

After those words, she barely uttered a sound as she slipped into the next world where Patsy, my grandparents, and my father were waiting to greet her. The room was strangely still and I realized that my life would sound forever different now that Lillian Sly had left it.

And the same is true about a good story as well. Once it's spoken, it permanently alters the way we listen to the next thing we hear or maybe it changes the way we love. However we are affected, it is in the telling of such things that will make us who we are for all to see. And, if we're lucky, it may also make someone fall in love with the shape of our lips or cause us to remember a beloved aunt who taught us the meaning of life.

ABOUT THE AUTHOR

Sias Bryant is a mixed bag of Midwest talent who is just beginning to make a ripple in the writing world. She is a storyteller and fierce lover of humanity who has had a hand in raising five amazing children; she is married to the woman who picked up her pieces and held them until she could find her way back to sanity; she is Elma and Eddie's daughter; she is Billy, Jimmy, and Nancy's surrogate sister; she is Steve and Scott's aunt; and she is Teri and Desiree's "ex." In short, she has had a life full of moments. In fact, her own story is likely to read like many of these remnants. Perhaps, one day, she may find the strength to write them into existence. Until then, she is grateful to have found support and encouragement for this offering in her editor, Carrie, and Nuance Books. She has stories in *Khimairal Ink* and *Blithe House Quarterly*.

You can email her at SBryant53@comcast.net

Printed in the United States
84670LV00002B/22/A

9 780975 955581